Meggie Albanesi

A Life in the Theatre

MEGGIE ALBANESI

A Life in the Theatre

Frances Gray

Society for Theatre Research
London

First published in 2010
by the Society for Theatre Research
PO Box 53971
London, SW15 6UL

ISBN 978 0 85430 076 1

General Editor: Professor Richard Foulkes

Volume Editor: Dr Kate Dorney

Printed and bound by CPI Antony Rowe, Chippenham, Wiltshire

For Alan, Rob, Dom, Sally and Kate

Contents

List of Illustrations

Illustrations from the Beryl Hoare collection in the Theatre & Performance department at the V&A, courtesy of V&A Images

Acknowledgements

This book has been a pleasure to write, which has a great deal to do with its subject, and I am happy to have spent time with Meggie Albanesi even at one remove. I am especially grateful to Phoebe Winch and Abby Hurden for family information and to Charles Lewsen and Gabriel Newfield who passed on some otherwise inaccessible details; Kathryn Johnson at the British Library for locating scripts; the staff of Sheffield University and Sheffield City Libraries who took so much trouble to unearth all kinds of material from the period; the staff of the V&A Theatre and Performance Department for programmes, reviews and photographs; Kristy Davis at the Mander and Mitchenson Collection; the staff of the Rylands Library for guiding me through the Basil Dean Archive; the University of Sheffield and the Society for Theatre Research for financial help; Kate Dorney, for things too numerous to mention; and the company who staged my own play on Meggie Albanesi and brought to life the work of many of the playwrights mentioned here: Alan Lane, Rob Hemus, Dominic Gately and Sally Proctor. I have given full acknowledgement to sources in the Notes section and made every reasonable effort to contact copyright holders; my apologies for any errors or omissions.

Run-through

'The first day of the week cometh Mary Magdalene to the tomb while it was yet dark…'

It is only a rehearsal. The actors wear their own clothes, curiously formal to modern eyes; this is the early 1920s. The elegant garments sort oddly with the countrified accents they have assumed for the play. It is morning, and they have matinees to perform, but instead of leaving when their parts are done they cluster in the stalls to watch the woman in the grey dress who is sitting at a kitchen table reading from St John's Gospel.

'For as yet they knew not the scripture, that he must rise again from the dead…'

The property clock strikes eight. This is the final scene, in which the man who has faithfully loved this woman and murdered her violent husband is hanged; she faces her ordeal alone except for his simple-minded brother huddled in her skirts.

'But Mary stood without at the sepulchre, weeping…'

The audience are weeping too. The voice is not beautiful; it is husky, even hoarse, a smoker's voice. But it enfolds them in its spell. They understand the woman's grief, her love, and her pride in the man who has confessed to save an innocent man from the gallows, her unshakeable religious faith. After the last line is spoken the applause comes, but first there is silence for a full minute, the silence that means that the audience cannot bear to part with the experience too soon.

A great actor in the right part can move and enchant time after time. Two people may be equally enchanted on two different nights; years later they may compare notes and enjoy the subtleties of their individual responses, and in doing so recapture some of the original pleasure. Sometimes, though, there is a performance that is an epiphany. The actor moves onto a different plane and the audience sense they are part of an event that can never be repeated. It strikes without warning. It may happen in front of thousands, or flash into being in a rehearsal room. The arbitrary nature of such an event can throw an actor into despair – Olivier, after a performance of Othello that stunned the company, fell into a towering rage at the thought that he could never repeat it. Sometimes, it partakes of something else, something numinous; a performance is quarried out of the last fragments of the actor's health and strength and its cost is reflected in its quality. Ian Charleson, dying of AIDS, his face and body visibly at their last extremity, played a final Hamlet in which he seemed to be reading despatches from the fringe of existence. As his friend and director Richard Eyre described it, 'He wasn't playing the part, he became the part.... his farewell and the character's agonisingly merged.'[1] The actors who watched the last run-through of *A Magdalen's Husband* were seeing such an

[1] Richard Eyre, *Utopia and Other Places* (Bloomsbury 1993), 132

event; they did not know it was the last performance, but they recognised the power of what they saw. The memory of it lasted more than fifty years.

They would never see even a shadow of it again. The woman in the grey dress, Meggie Albanesi, died three days later. She was twenty-four.

It was the start of an era that would become accustomed to great acting: the age of Gielgud and Olivier, Richardson and Redgrave, Guinness and Laughton, Evans and Ashcroft. Over the next fifty years there would be new styles, new writers, new media, and new opportunities that this remarkable generation forged for themselves. Meggie Albanesi was the vanguard – role model, rival, a co-star to dream of. She asked the same questions, challenged the same conventions, and shaped the new kind of acting they demanded. Death robbed her of the status and the fame of her contemporaries; it also deprived the theatre of her distinctive contribution to that crucible of talent. Most of those who followed her in the next few years uncovered their true powers in classical theatre as Romeo or Millamant or Hamlet. Meggie had talked about the major roles, had discussed Ibsen's Nora with a director, wondered if the existing translations of Chekhov would do; more than once, she studied Juliet with more experienced friends and some thought she would define the role for her generation. But her uniqueness lay in her ability to show the youth of the twenties to itself, even though the painful struggles to define that self had barely begun when she died.

Meggie Albanesi embodied the clear-sighted bitterness of post-war youth in *A Bill of Divorcement*, the most talked-about play of 1921. *A Magdalen's Husband,* chosen as a vehicle in which she might achieve the same tragic force, tries for the timeless rural rhythms of Thomas Hardy; but in 1923, the year that saw the execution of Edith Thompson, it spoke of crime and sexuality, love and death, stirring powerful emotions in an audience who found themselves asking questions about the English justice system and the place of women. Rehearsing this role by day, Meggie was dancing her way each night through the hit comedy of the year as a silly young flapper suddenly confronted with real love. To all these facets of her own generation she brought a unique truth, utterly unforced but with a power that gave every role a core of sincerity and steel. But while she could embody like nobody else the painful changes of the 1920s, she was also a casualty of them. She took terrible risks. So did many of her contemporaries, and they survived and learned and went on living. But, as Meggie once said to her mother, she had great luck, but she was not lucky.

The other stars of her generation lived into vigorous old age. If there are few alive who saw Olivier's fiery, controversial and realistic Romeo in 1935 or Gielgud's Trofimov in an England still perplexed by Chekhov in 1924, there are many who remember their energetic middle years. And thanks to the technological innovations that took place in those long lifetimes, they could work till the end. In 1988, nine months before his death, Olivier recited Wilfred Owen's *Strange Meeting* for the Derek Jarman film *War Requiem*. Gielgud celebrated his 96th birthday in 2000 working on a film of Beckett's *Catastrophe,* days before he died. Film, tape and video have ensured that many of their performances are accessible to coming generations.

These can mislead: as fashions alter, in dress, in diction, in style, the performer on celluloid changes for us: the body seems the wrong shape, the voice too clipped, the gestures overblown, the make-up a mask. But a great performer on film can also surprise. When the codes governing the performance have changed, it becomes apparent that some actors had a genuine dependency, but others were using them as a flourish on something more individual grounded deeply in themselves. The possibility of defining the nature of this individuality may be diminished since their deaths, but it is nonetheless there.

There are no surviving films of Meggie Albanesi. She worked on a handful of silent movies, but within a few years most of them were superseded by talking remakes. Her only substantial film, Sjöstrom's *Honour,* seems to have vanished. It is impossible to catch at the nature of her art that way. We are deprived of the chance just as we are deprived of stage encounters which never took place but which, given a few more years, would have been almost inevitable. No one will ever see Albanesi challenge Olivier, the two most powerful pairs of eyes in the theatre sharing a stage; or watch her dreaming onstage with Richardson, who said when he was approaching old age that 'her brilliance might have outshone all…not many can remember her now, though I for one forever will;'[2] she can never be seen performing opposite Gielgud, who watched her in his student days with passionate though critical admiration and annotated programmes with his memories; or on film with Victor Sjöstrom; hence we have also lost the opportunity to see them differently too, subtly changed by their experience of her. We can never have the memory of her as an elderly performer at the RSC or the National, imparting her power to a new generation of actors; with her commitment to creating new roles by new writers, we have lost her interactions with generations of playwrights from Brecht to Churchill. Nor did she reach an age at which she might have been moved to articulate in detail her own approach to performance, her sense of her own life and its direction.

Without her, though, the history of that starry generation of performers is incomplete. And what we do have is enough, perhaps, to go some way towards reconstructing the stage presence of an extraordinary woman. There may be only fragments of her life left to us, but they can be given a context; we can read them in terms of the theatrical cross-currents of her time, the choices available to her and the things that were there to be learned. And they can be told in an order; the scraps can be surveyed and assembled and made into narrative. Narrative frees up the imagination that is always at work in theatre history, that of a reading audience, never directly addressed by the performer who has long ceased to speak, but discovering that there is still an exchange going on across the deserted footlights.

There are at least some resources with which to construct a narrative. First, there are photographs. Sometimes it can be an uphill task to try to extrapolate a widely admired performance from photographs; lively and respected actors can seem curiously stiff in pictures only a few years old, stuck at the mid-point of gestures which seem to lack spontaneity, the momentary passage of a thought or an emotion frozen on the face. Meggie's photographs look as if she might turn and speak any second, as if her stillness is of her own choosing and she might be willing to break it for us.

Then there are descriptions of her in performance; while some critics offered only unhelpful superlatives there were those who watched more closely. They tried to articulate what made her different from her contemporaries, to relate her work to European acting traditions that seemed to provide closer models of her art. They were alert to developments, so that one-off reviews often partake of the nature of a running commentary. There are records by those who worked alongside her; she had

---

[2] Ralph Richardson Archive, British Library MS Department. My thanks to Dr Kate Dorney for a sight of Richardson's draft speech to mark the retirement of Basil Dean, in which this appears

a keen sense of what she needed to learn, and what she could draw from every opportunity. T.P. O'Connor, then Father of the House of Commons and a man passionately committed to the future of British theatre, noted in her epitaph the sense among the theatre community that Meggie Albanesi was their responsibility. 'Nobody grudged her success, everybody wanted to help her…she was regarded as something rather outside the customary rivals and jealousies.'[3]

In a brief career she worked within a broad stylistic spectrum – the last embers of the actor-manager tradition, commercial fluff, experimental companies that kept European innovation alive in Sunday performances and matinees in a climate shy of the new, many of them run by women. They were all the best of their kind; they all offered her something new to learn. There were those who documented the process because it was vital to their own sense of themselves, who knew that their lives and careers had been changed.

In particular, there was the company of which she became the symbol and figurehead, ReandeaN, based at the St Martin's Theatre. Committed to annihilating the split between commercial and experimental theatre, ReandeaN's aims were unlike any other group in London; it was not always successful and it did not last; there were mistakes, struggles, clashes of personality, but also a working atmosphere in which moments like that scene at the kitchen table could grow. It was a forcing house for her talent and its history is almost inextricable from her own. And – part of that same company's history – there are texts written with her in mind by writers who also strove to embody their century. Behind the words you can catch a glimpse of a personal Meggie Albanesi – Galsworthy's, Clemence Dane's, Coward's – ghosts of performances charged with powers the authors knew were there and were convinced they could bring out.

Her memorial is on the wall of the St Martin's, a relief by Eric Gill. Based on a studio portrait, it is stylised into a bland classical format, the body curved with elegance but no muscular power and the profile beautiful but expressionless. Only the hands are individual, large and capable, the hands of a worker or a musician. Despite its grace it is less arresting than the photographs. Meggie was a performer above all, and it was only in performance that her vitality shone out.

For years now the identity of the St Martin's has been bound up with *The Mousetrap*. Theatregoers who pass the image on the wall, intent on spotting the murderer of Monkswell Manor, may wonder, but they will not remember. But the figure on the plaque was part of an episode of theatre history too important to forget, and possessed of a talent that needs a more vital place in the memory than stone can give.

---

[3] E. Maria Albanesi, *Meggie Albanesi* (Hodder and Stoughton 1928), 149

Nineteenth-century start
1899–1916

She was a Victorian, one of a generation with mixed feelings about that label and its heritage. Margherita Cecilia Brigida Lucia Maria Albanesi was born on the afternoon of Sunday, 8 October 1899, the day before the Boer War broke out. In 1931 her friend and contemporary Noel Coward began his state-of-the-nation play *Cavalcade* at this same point. Disingenuously, he claimed this was the result of an arbitrary decision to research the year of his birth in the *Illustrated London News* and that he might have chosen 'the storming of the Winter Palace at St Petersburg'[4]; but he knew he had picked a liminal moment. The first lullaby crooned over Meggie's cradle by her nurse was one of Kipling's ambiguous Service Songs, aggressively asserting the virtues of Empire but warning that

> He's an absent-minded beggar and he may forget it all,
> But we do not want his kiddies to remind him
> That we sent 'em to the workhouse while their daddy hammered Paul...[5]

The mixture of swaggering jingoism and guilt, the uncomfortable awareness of the poverty and ill-health of the British fighting man made it a fitting anthem to the last imperial adventure, rapidly bogged down in frustration and failure. Meggie's generation of artists, growing up with this ambivalent political consciousness alongside the optimism born of innovations like the cinema and the motor car, all experienced a need to give the times new shape and definition, and they were to make the theatre a very different place from that of the old century.

'Albanesi' means 'Albanian'. The first Albanesis came to Southern Italy as mercenaries in the service of King Alfonso of Aragon; in return the Aragonese protected them from the Turks and offered them a safe haven after the massacre of Otranto in 1480; they flooded into the city of Naples and flourished; today the surname is one of the most common in the city. Carlo Albanesi, Meggie's father, was a Neapolitan, born in October 1858. The exotic air that clusters about his name, as foreign in his own land as his adopted one, is reflected in dramatic looks; the exceptionally large dark eyes, the strong nose and the wide mobile mouth were all passed to his daughter. His branch of the Albanesi clan was lively and successful, one brother a judge, another a doctor, and a sister married to the painter Oscar Richard.

Carlo dabbled in watercolour and collected art, but his own field was music. He studied piano under yet another member of the clan, Luigi Albanesi. He made a name for himself as a musician in Italy and Paris, arriving in 1882 in an England

---

[4] *Daily Mail*, 8 Sept 1960
[5] Kipling, *The Absent-Minded Beggar,* Complete Verse (Kyle Cathie 1990), 366

beglamoured by Garibaldi and all things Italian. An instant success on the concert platform, he was awarded a Chair at the Royal Academy of Music in 1893.

At this point he gave up performing. He had a busy schedule, teaching violin and piano at the Academy, with a number of private pupils including the princesses of Connaught, Daisy and Patsy; he was in demand as an examiner for various musical institutions and composed for piano and orchestra. Why he chose to give up the concert platform is not clear. It may be that he just wanted a more ordered routine. The rhythms of his teaching life were highly structured and this caused domestic clashes later.

Her mother was a more pacific character. She was born Effie Maria Henderson in 1859. Her origins are mysterious and for some years her birth date was wrongly recorded as 1864; she was rumoured to be one of three illegitimate daughters of Marie Sadleir, the widow of an army officer and the second child of the songwriter Sydney Nelson. If so, Nelson, the author of some 800 ballads and comic operas for the Lyceum, bequeathed her the popular touch. She earned a good living as a romantic novelist, cashing in on the upsurge of cheaply produced fiction in the latter half of the nineteenth century.

Her industry was prodigious. From 1886 she produced a steady stream of novelettes in soft paper covers decorated with images of young women in noble attitudes; at her death in 1936 she had over 250 publications to her name, and more prepared for posthumous publication. Most were under her favoured pseudonym, Effie Adelaide Rowlands, although some bore the name E. Maria Albanesi, including her own biography of Meggie.

She knew her market. Sixpenny novels (or dime novels in the USA, where her agent – the first of such in the UK, A.P. Watt – negotiated for her very successfully) were regarded as beneath the dignity of middle-class lending libraries like Boots and Mudie's; but they were in demand among young women in factories or domestic service, working long hours and starved of both male company and a wage that would permit independence. They liked their texts short, around fifteen thousand words, easy to carry on the bus; they liked heroines tough but virtuous. Rowlands heroines were fresh, sweet and resourceful; they were kind to old ladies and children and navigated vicissitudes from orphanhood to pretend engagements with impeccable manners; villainesses revealed themselves by such gestures as striking matches on the soles of their high-heeled shoes to light their cigarettes. What gave Effie Rowlands the edge over her competitors was the relish she brought to anecdotes of children (one of her heroes shows himself an all-round good guy by climbing into a bath in his best suit so his little cousins can play Nanny) and to ordinary sensuous pleasures like this snatch of landscape:

> A broad clear light fell upon the orchard...discovering the harvest of fallen apples (a veritable feast later for the old sow and her nine piglets) catching the glint of the brook that ran in the distance, and making the thousands of mushrooms spread themselves into a soft, creamwhite carpet.[6]

That competitive edge is apparent on the cover of Street and Smith's Newstrade Bulletin depicting their 'best girl' customer surrounded by vignettes of her favourite authors, including Rowlands herself. It is equally apparent in Dorothy Richardson's

---

[6] *Susannah and One Elder,* (Methuen 1903), 3

account of factory girls in New York, *The Long Day*: Richardson tried to woo them off Rowlands and onto Dickens only to be sent away with a flea in her ear.[7]

Rowlands also found literary champions. The often acid Max Beerbohm was not greatly impressed with her attempt to dramatise one of her novels, *Susannah – And Some Others* ('I have yet to see a woman's play in which the male characters shall seem real and vital') but he gave her credit for lively dialogue and awarded an accolade most romance writers would treasure: 'It is *not sugary*.'[8] The situations might be contrived, but the novels were not cynical; they expressed Effie Maria's own sentiments about life. As the market foundered after the First World War she knew she was out of sync with changing mores, but stuck to the tradition she understood, wryly noting that she might seem too 'pretty-pretty'; her craftsmanship carried her through where others fell by the wayside.

The marriage seems to have been successful but it had its strains. Carlo could be hot-tempered, one of those people calm in a major crisis but raging at minor upsets: his family nickname was 'Fierce One'. Effie also hints that Carlo could rock the relationship to an almost intolerable degree:

> In my opinion both Meggie and her father were two of the most honourable people I have ever met, but they were strangely lacking in discrimination in connection with certain associations which crept now and then into their lives. One can fight an enemy openly, but it is awfully difficult to fight elements of deceit, and underhand doings, and subtlety.[9]

Whatever the personal matters at issue, Effie never abandoned the euphemistic style of her romance novels. She refused to speak openly about difficulties, on the pretext of protecting Carlo, to whom she never mentioned Meggie and Eva's inevitable childhood accidents and illnesses. Keeping her mouth shut was her coping strategy, and there were facts about her daughter she would neither acknowledge nor articulate. They were, however, an affectionate family. Effie was sole carer in her children's earliest days. While Meggie and her sister Eva were still toddlers her parents took a farmhouse in Kent for use in the spring and summer and Carlo's regular weekend arrival from London was a matter for celebration.

Effie's descriptions of country life resemble Kate Greenaway illustrations; there are scenes of Meggie and Eva tumbling about with piglets and lambs, grooming shire horses and driving geese, running to meet Father in the governess cart, getting muddy with local children declared 'rough' and off-limits. It is a picture in pastels, more than a little sentimental. Effie admitted using anecdotes about her children in her novels and the strategy cut both ways; at times, she seems to read her daughters' behaviour and her expectations of them through a lens of remorseless romance.

However, these pastoral images of childhood also demonstrate willingness to let the girls graze their knees and yell their heads off – a more tomboy existence than many girls of the period enjoyed. Meggie liked boys' adventure stories and she and Eva turned the nursery into a battleship and fought with walking stick swords; on trips to the park they drove the maid to distraction with their imaginary pets – ten fierce dogs, each with its own whip-cracking signal.

---

[7] See *American Women's Dime Novel Project*,http://chnm.gmu.edu.dimenovels/intro.html
[8] Max Beerbohm, *Last Theatres 1904–1910* (Rupert Hart-Davis, 1970), 338–10
[9] *Meggie Albanesi,* 101

Effie and Carlo worked long hours; but they liked the presence of the children and much of their education was at home. At the farm a woman with theories about child-rearing was their first carer after the nurse, and bullied Effie into disposing of a battered doll to which both girls were devoted; then a local woman gave them lessons; in London they went to a local school and to the Convent of Our Lady of Sion for instruction in their father's Catholic faith. Lessons were supplemented by French and German governesses and instruction in fencing, swimming and riding. Meggie responded best to these and never lost her pleasure in them. Eva was more academic, with a real talent for art; she liked learning in a class and opted to go back to school. Meggie struggled with lessons and it was with her German governess that she got most of her organised education.

In the house in Mandeville Place where the Albanesis spent the winter there were opportunities for less formal learning. Musicians, writers and performers were part of the social circle and they were not the kind who expected children to be seen and not heard. The girls met Caruso and Clara Butt; they were petted by their neighbour Tosti, the composer. Artists sketched them and noted Eva's developing talent for drawing. They were in demand at parties. Everybody played for them to dance, (although they favoured Carlo's improvisations for them on the piano). James Douglas recalls a children's party where he met an eleven-year-old Meggie looking like 'a neglected glow-worm',[10] downcast because nobody had admired her party frock. Her disappointment was on the frock's behalf rather than for herself; it was, she confided, by Bakst, whose designs for the Ballets Russes were currently taking London by storm.

There were naturally trips to the theatre, although this was a rationed treat; Meggie became almost ill with excitement at her first outing, to see *The Water Babies* – evidently a very striking production. Eva went to one of the first performances of *Peter Pan* in 1904, with Nina Boucicault spooky and sinister as the boy who wouldn't grow up, but it was seen as too powerful for Meggie, not yet five. They were enthusiastic home performers, Eva taking responsibility for the set, programmes and script (sometimes helped by the Curtis Brown children, whose parents ran the literary agency) and Meggie in the starring role.

At five she appeared in public for the first time at a performance by the Pastoral Players in the Botanical Gardens, dressed as Cupid in a proper theatrical wig of golden curls. A bigger opportunity came in 1908 when Herbert Trench brought Maeterlinck's *Blue Bird* to the Haymarket, and suggested that Meggie might play Tyltyl. Four years previously the Vaudeville had seen a starry cast and luscious production values in the first London performance of *Pelleas and Melisande* and Trench had every intention of matching the style if not the gloomy symbolism; it offered a high-profile debut in an efficiently organised Christmas spectacular. Carlo, however, sensibly considered that a project of such magnitude should not be placed on the shoulders of an eight-year-old and vetoed the idea. Trench eventually agreed and a young actress called Olive Walters played the part.

It was, clearly, a privileged childhood; but perhaps the greatest piece of good fortune was the determination of Carlo and Effie that their daughters should do something worthwhile. The Sex Disqualification (Removal) Act was some years off. Women were still legally barred from several of the professions and venturing into others with grave difficulty. The outlook for the daughter of well-off parents might be financially brighter than her working-class counterparts, but in terms of

[10] *Sunday Express*, 16 Dec 1923

job satisfaction her options were limited. Cynthia Asquith, entering the adult world while Meggie was making her first theatre trips as a toddler, recalled that 'for a girl to go to university was a deviation from the normal almost as wide as taking the veil, or, by a stride in the other direction, going on the stage.'[11]

The Albanesis, however, seemed to assume that their daughters would and should go into the arts. The seriousness with which they approached their training meant that in one sense they were more fortunate than girls who had to struggle for their ambitions to be taken seriously. On the other hand, both were reared in a house where it was taken for granted that 'work' involved endless rehearsal, drafts and re-drafts, and that it meant above all preparing yourself to be judged: by an audience, by a readership. Eva, although she liked to write, chose a new sphere, and attended the Slade. Originally it was assumed that Meggie would be a musician like her father, and at ten she began to study the violin.

She had a musician's hands, spanning more than an octave with strong fingers; some people called them mannish. Her tutor, Rowsby Woof, thought they were 'wonderful violin hands' and that her work was promising. She was not altogether comfortable with the arrangement; the piano was her second instrument, and she turned to it more and more. Eventually she taught herself some technically demanding pieces by Scriabin and played them to Woof at the Royal Academy. He agreed that 'nature intended her to be a pianist'.[12] Meggie went to the Royal Academy of Music, into her father's class.

It was, predictably, a disaster. The situation put them both under pressure. Her situation marked her out from the other students; his put him in a position where he had to prove himself as a teacher in a new way. She had talent, but perhaps not enough; or maybe he felt obliged to be harder on his daughter. She needed to take things at her own pace and Carlo's patience wore thin. Then she had a minor illness. Effie considered it providential, an excuse to withdraw with honour intact on both sides. Meggie, however, was devastated at her failure. For the rest of her life, in the teeth of all the evidence to the contrary, she assumed that she had failed to meet expectations. Rehearsal made her happy; first nights hardly ever did.

By this time, the war had disrupted her education. The German governess, as Effie puts it, 'disappeared', voluntarily or otherwise, and it was no longer deemed appropriate to speak or study German. She had nothing to focus her energy and was profoundly depressed. Effie suggested a possible solution: her friend Beryl Faber had always praised Meggie's talent in the plays she devised with Eva, and the Academy of Dramatic Art (not yet Royal) might accept her as a student. The idea brought an instant response, and she auditioned as soon as she had mastered the set pieces.

[11] Cited Nicola Beauman, *Cynthia Asquith* (Hamish Hamilton 1987)
[12] *Meggie Albanesi,* 39

'The imagination is guided'

1916–1917

ADA was an adventurous choice for a performer who wanted some kind of training. Only a few years before she would probably have joined one of the few companies that took their responsibilities to the novice seriously enough to develop a school, like Frank Benson's. Or she might have chosen a private tutor, like the American teacher Hermann Vezin. Or she could have attended one of the music academies with classes in operatic skills. All of these continued to flourish and produced some of the leading actors of the period.

Carlo's own position, however, would have made him aware of the new enthusiasm for a major centre of actor training with the status as his own institution, something analogous to the French Conservatoire. Two schools with this level of ambition had opened: ADA, founded by Sir Herbert Beerbohm Tree in 1904, had the edge of seniority over the Central School of Speech and Drama, founded by Elsie Fogerty in 1906.

ADA had already emerged from its original exciting but inconvenient location at Tree's own theatre, His Majesty's, to a pair of houses in Gower Street. Tree had given over its control to a council whose composition made its aspirations clear. First, it offered graduates a chance of work with no less than five working actor-managers: Tree, Irene Vanbrugh, Sir Johnston Forbes Robertson, Cyril Maude, Sir George Alexander, and Arthur Bourchier. Second, it offered insights into the working world of theatre at its best, with Shaw, Sir James Barrie, Sir Arthur Wing Pinero and Sir W.S. Gilbert giving time not just to council affairs but to rehearsing their own plays with the students. And, with the retired theatre veterans Sir Squire Bancroft and Sir John Hare swelling the clutch of knighthoods, it offered respectability previous generations had not dreamed of.

Many of the students were well-to-do; others, like Meggie's close friend Molly Lumley, were the children of actors, encouraged by a reduction in the twelve guinea fee; all were at home with the codes of deportment underpinning the Bancrofts' own 'gentrification' of the rumbustious Victorian theatre. The staff were alert to the concern that ADA might become a finishing school, especially as female applicants outnumbered male by four to one. The policy of the Administrator, Kenneth Barnes, was to reflect as far as possible the opportunities available in the professional theatre. Men had an easier time auditioning, so that they were outnumbered only two to one.

However, the onset of war shifted this balance. Meggie's year was all female. It is unfortunate that economic necessity and the need to do his bit at the front deprived her of the opportunity to work with her exact contemporary Charles Laughton, twenty-four when he finally reached RADA. But, on the whole, the absence of men may have proved empowering in a way that a mixed if unbalanced intake could not. Unless there is consciously adventurous cross-casting, a limited number of men will ensure that women are cast in male roles – but not the central, challenging ones; rather, a minor male role becomes an invitation to self-effacement, to avoid drawing attention to the incongruity. This may explain why C.M. Lowne, the Administrator while Barnes was at the Front, felt that Meggie's class was exceptional, 'one of the best the Academy had ever had'.[13] There were real opportunities there for the taking.

ADA still had a ramshackle, improvised air. The theatre, as Dodie Smith, a student in 1914, recalls

> had been made by knocking down the dividing wall between the two houses and replacing it with a curtain. The stage was raised in the drawing room of one house, the auditorium was in the drawing-room of the other; and beyond this another wall had been knocked down so that a little back room could serve as what was known as the Royal Box, for the Administrator and distinguished guests.[14]

If architecturally unconventional, it was well supplied with rehearsal space, a floor fit to train dancers and a long low basement , the social centre of the place where sandwiches and iced buns were dispensed by an enormous woman called Henry.

The training it offered was primarily technical. Tree was aware of his physical and vocal shortcomings while learning his trade in amateur companies and he well understood that the new London theatres under construction were larger than before, making heavy demands on the voice,[15] especially in view of the more natural and unforced acting styles becoming fashionable. Tree nominated 'voice production and elocution' first when interviewed about the curriculum on the eve of ADA's opening; speech courses are the first to be named in the first term syllabus.

Elocution was taught by a Tree company veteran, A.E.George, 'a small man with a tremendous voice',[16] who also taught Shakespeare. Ballet and dance were taught by Louis Hervey D'Egville. His family had for generations run a famous private studio in Conduit Street, where the socially ambitious came for instruction in dancing and deportment; D'Egville imparted not only flexibility but a high gloss which gave his students the confidence to play aristocratic characters and cope fluently with period style and clothing. Students were expected to perform in French, and Alice Gachet, responsible for this part of the curriculum, also had an eye for potential; she would select students for less immediately obvious roles to bring it out – Laughton considered that she changed his life and liked to cite her comment, 'I will break your heart, but I will make an artist of you.' [17]

There was, from the second term, a process of continual rehearsal; students whizzed through about forty different characters in a year, inducted into their roles by working actors in a haphazard fashion that sometimes worked and sometimes did not. Helen Haye, later to work with Meggie in *The Skin Game*, imparted some valuable emotional discipline in sessions Flora Robson called 'Hell with Helen'[18], insisting that every speech contained one climactic moment and one only; but often she simply demonstrated how she would play a scene, so that 'the entire stage was

---

[13] *Meggie Albanesi*, 47
[14] Dodie Smith, *Look Back with Mixed Feelings* (London 1978), 36
[15] Michael Sanderson, *From Irving to Olivier (*Athlone Press 1984), 33
[16] Smith, *Look Back,* 40
[17] Simon Callow, *Charles Laughton: A Difficult Actor* (Methuen 1988), 12
[18] Margaret McCall (ed.), *My Drama School* (Robson Books 1978), 30

peopled with little Helen Hayes.'[19] Every actor's memories of the Academy seem to include the 'Jonsonian'[20] figure of Elsie Chester, whose acting career had ended with the loss of a leg, and who taught modern drama with a ferocity that sometimes led her to hurl her crutches at weak performers. Rosina Filippi, the half-sister of Duse, who had worked with Benson and Tree, was the best woman teacher of the day and had run her own studio for some years before ADA recruited her; motherly, untidy and blunt, surrounded by clouds of dogs and cigarette smoke and waving a fencing foil to emphasise a point, she was a close friend of Shaw, who came to watch her work on his plays. Despite the apparently random style of her class – she might carry on a conversation at the same time – her main emphasis was on the combination of clear and musical speech, 'full vowels and sharp consonants'[21] with flexibility of movement a Shavian performer needs. While Filippi might leap onstage and perform by way of illustration, this was a way of galvanising the student rather than eliciting carbon copies; her strength lay in the way she could communicate her own passion for the work to students, just as she tried to communicate a passion for Shakespeare to the patrons of a struggling Old Vic.

What was on offer, in short, was a grounding in technique allied to the possibility of inspiration on a rather random basis, arising out of individual encounters between the student, the tutor and the role. The advice sprang from solid experience; the sample performance provided an opportunity to observe in close focus, to learn from it in a way that could not happen in the theatre. As a teaching technique this kind of master class could work as long as the teacher recognised the potential of each student and, even more important, if the student had the courage to reject suggestions that did not work for her personally.

What was not yet on offer was a clear programme of instruction in the art of acting, one that explored the emotional crosscurrents of a text and the actor's inner resources. This had not been a felt need in the early years: now some of the new generation were beginning to articulate a sense of lack. Eva le Gallienne, a student confidante of Meggie (she had been drawn to acting by that same production of *The Water Babies*), was to pioneer civic repertory theatre in America in the thirties; she recalls giving a passionate reading of Juliet at the audition stage of an ADA production only to crash in flames when the part was hers. 'I had no technique of emotion, and it was beyond my power to recapture the agony of grief that had somehow poured through me at that first attempt.'[22] Her experience is endorsed by Peggy Ashcroft, a pupil at Central in 1924, who recalls the avidity with which actors fell upon Stanislavsky's *My Life in Art* when it appeared that year in the UK and offered a disciplined way of organising and refreshing the emotional energies needed for a role.[23]

Meanwhile, however, there was one innovation on the ADA curriculum, the system of exercises devised by François Delsarte. While earlier methods laid down prescribed gestures for actors portraying specific emotional responses, Delsarte aimed at restoring spontaneity. Children, he maintained, were fluent and expressive with their bodies but straitjacketed by conventions until they expressed personal relationships through words alone, their only confident physical self-expression confined to the way they dealt with objects. For him, emotions and thoughts not

---

[19] Fabia Drake, *Blind Fortune* (Kimber 1978), 24
[20] Drake, 2
[21] Cathleen Nesbitt, *A Little Love and Good Company,* (Faber 1975), 47
[22] Eva le Gallienne, *At 33* (John Lane, Bodley Head 1934), 80
[23] Michael Billington, *Peggy Ashcroft* (John Murray 1988), 20

translated into physical movement generated muscular tensions from which the body needed liberation. His exercises were not designed to impose a preordained shape on the body, as in ballet, but to develop the physical resources of the individual and forge pathways between expression and emotion. 'The body becomes alive to the feeling within [and] imagination is quickened. The student becomes aware of forces within himself.'[24]

Delsarte exercises offered a warm-up for the whole body; they helped to develop a flexibility that, as Michael Sanderson points out, contrasts with the rigid and corseted inhibitions expected of young women born into late Victorian society.[25] More than this, Delsarte encouraged the relaxation and balance Stanislavsky also saw as the vital neutral gear for the performing body engaged by the physical and emotional demands of a role. If D'Egville's training supplied formal grace, Delsarte made the actor aware of the body's everyday relationship to gravity and surrounding space. The occasionally mystical language in which the exercises are described, the 'spiritual' and 'mental' spiral movements supposed to engender lofty or earthy feelings, is sometimes dense and clotted, as Stanislavsky's prose can be. But it also has some of the same effect – to allow the actor to understand what he is doing from within rather than making a set of mechanical responses.

Production photographs often show Meggie in a state of stillness, the body in neutral; they are also full of meaning, unencumbered by the stiff gestures often going on all round her; there is an innate rightness about the way she places herself on the stage, about the poise of the head and the way the eyes are precisely focused, so that the character's thought seems about to be born in speech without any conscious intervention in the process. If she missed the Method, she still had access to a training that could give her what she needed.

Delsarte was a bold choice for the ADA curriculum, and not everyone appreciated it or taught it well. Seniors were resentful when Ethel McGlinchy, a particularly flexible eleven-year-old generally known as The Shrimp, was brought in from the lower school to demonstrate her mastery of it; she was to become a friend and protegée of Meggie (who as ADA fencing champion presumably did not feel threatened). McGlinchy had arrived at ADA aged nine; she specialised in male roles – she played Henry V for ANZAC troops, though her favourite part was Cardinal Richelieu in heavy false whiskers; at thirteen she was Toby Belch to the Maria of ten-year-old Laurence Olivier, perhaps the only school play every theatre historian regrets missing. Her name changed to the more euphonious ' Fabia Drake', she worked with distinguished companies including ReandeaN, vindicating the ADA policy of cross casting as a liberating experience.

Meggie's own most notable piece of cross-casting, as the French marine officer Duvallet in Shaw's *Fanny's First Play*, had valuable learning potential, especially if Shaw's fondness for a hands-on approach to his work for the ADA council was in evidence. The role did not have much emotional content but embodied the youthful spirit of the play. First performed in 1911, it was Shaw's most popular success to date, a fizzy and topical celebration of youth. Two children of conventional families have their expectations of life shaken after they separately spend a fortnight in jail; they renounce their stodgy engagement – he, to marry a prostitute, she a footman (who inevitably turns out to be the socialist offspring of a

[24] Rose O'Neill, *Delsarte: The Science and Art of Speech and Gesture* (C.W.Daniel 1927), 38
[25] Sanderson, *Irving to Olivier,* 43

duke). It is left to Duvallet to articulate the meaning of these changes. In a speech a full three pages long he sings the praises of modern England.

> 'Where else are women trained to box and knock out the teeth of policemen as a protest against injustice and violence? [E]verywhere in these islands one can enjoy the exhilarating, the soul-liberating spectacle of women quarrelling with their brothers, defying their fathers, refusing to speak to their mothers...' [26]

The speech is a large responsibility for an actor, full of paradox and argument needing careful navigation. Duvallet boasts he can 'kick like a windmill' and exuberant demonstration is called for. While the speech had always been the climax of the play, the revival gave it new resonance: the eulogy to England is earthed with flip conceits about common sense versus French idealism, but in the wartime context it was a patriotic showstopper, an attractive opportunity for any student and one Meggie, in a natty borrowed suit, exploited to the full.

At the Annual Public Performance, a production under professional conditions at the New Theatre before leading actors and potential employers, she had a more orthodox opportunity; she was cast as Lady Teazle. Although a major role it was also a hazardous one; Lady Teazle is seventeen, like Meggie herself; character parts, like Mrs Candour (played by her friend Mollie Lumley) provide a kind of safety; they allow the actor to show off skills, cover up some bodily faults and sink uncertainties into a very different persona. By contrast, Lady Teazle offers no place to hide. The role demands all the D'Egville skills with fans and curtseys; the prose is lucid but often convoluted; it takes powerful vocal control to navigate sentences like 'As for that smooth-tongued hypocrite who would have seduced the wife of his too credulous friend, while he affected honourable addresses to his ward – I behold him now in a light so truly despicable that I shall never again respect myself for having listened to him.'

However, it also requires a sexy innocence that depends on personal charisma and the ability to show a personality changing as Lady Teazle undergoes moral growth. While the role is that of a naive character, reacting to situations rather than initiating them, the actor controls the stage much of the time. It is her timing, her instinct when to peep out from hiding or to bring forth a character in the background, on which the pace and rhythm of the action depend. Like Juliet, it is a role which demands too much of an actress the correct age to play it.

Meggie missed a number of rehearsals. She had chicken pox, a serious illness once childhood is over; the stress was compounded by the fact that her own doctor was away at the front. However, the locum pulled her through, though she was still shakily convalescent on the day. Effie provided an eighteenth-century gown and powdered Meggie's own luxuriant hair (costumes were always a worry to ADA students: they had to supply these and the less well off found it a struggle, although staff could be generous in lending their own). One member of the audience left a brief review which suggests the energy and spirit she brought to a role that could have been bland in the midst of more overtly comic characters: 'No one could be blind to the charm, the sensitiveness, the pathos and the emotional power manifest in her acting.'[27] She left the theatre, worn out, as soon as the performance was over,

---

[26] Shaw, *Fanny's First Play* (Constable 1914), 221
[27] Malcolm Watson, cited Albanesi 17

and it was up to her fellow students to phone her and report that the judges, Johnston Forbes Robertson, Irene Vanbrugh and Sir John Hare, had unanimously awarded her ADA's chief accolade, the Bancroft Gold Medal. In those days it was made of real gold.

'Small-fry'
1917–1918

Some debuts are disastrous, some brilliant. Meggie Albanesi's was respectable. The play, *A Pair of Spectacles*, was a stolid Victorian comedy older than she was; its premiere was in 1890. The author, Sydney Grundy, had vehemently opposed Ibsen and the New Drama and persistently attacked the playwrights of the new century until he died in 1914. The star, Sir John Hare of the Gold Medal board, was a member of the Advisory Board to the Lord Chamberlain and his advice was always on the safe side: he had 'grave doubts' about licensing a translation of *Oedipus* on the grounds that it would 'probably…lead to a great number of plays being written and submitted to the censor appealing to a vitiated public taste solely in the course of indecency'.[28]

Benjamin Goldfinch, the hero who borrows the eponymous spectacles and is briefly transformed into a miser, was Hare's most famous role, and he emerged from retirement to reprise it for one of the charity performances that characterised wartime London. This one trailed extra clouds of respectability in the shape of the most beloved members of the Royal Family. On 23 July 1917 Queen Alexandra and the Princess Royal arrived at the Haymarket, complete with a guard of honour from the training ship HMS *Arethusa*. The audience had stumped up a thousand pounds in aid of King George's Fund for Sailors, and were in sentimental mood, applauding Hare until he tearfully declared in his curtain speech that 'you have spoiled me all my life,'[29] and thanked his 'brilliantly clever' cast. This included Kate Rorke as Mrs Goldfinch (a part she had played on and off since 1890), and his former protégé Gerald Du Maurier, to whom he had given his first professional role in 1894. The success of the day moved Du Maurier to return the compliment by bringing the production into his own theatre, Wyndham's, where it opened on 1 September.

Although a speaking part in the West End is an achievement in itself for an actress not yet eighteen, it was not a production that would bring Meggie much notice. It was an exercise in nostalgia, indulged right down to an ancient tradition other theatres had abandoned, a decorative border around all four sides of the Wyndham's stage to reinforce the sense of an old-fashioned picture book.

The reviews responded to the aim of the show rather than performances; they focussed on the fun of the reunion between the 73-year-old Hare and Du Maurier, playing his young scapegrace nephew at the age of forty-four, and celebrated the talent that had sustained Hare's long career – that of radiating cosiness. 'We cannot bear Benjamin Goldfinch to be unhappy, suspicious, disappointed,' announced *The Times,* 'because Sir John Hare has made Benjamin Goldfinch as much our own dear

---

[28] Nicholas de Jongh, *Politics, Prudery and Perversions: the Censoring of the English Stage 1901–1968* (Methuen 2000), 52

[29] *The Times*, 24 July 1917

friend as if he were "real".' The rest of the cast, it noted, 'did what they had to do with a promise, at least, of the finish Wyndham's Theatre has inherited from Sir John Hare's Garrick Theatre of the 1890s' – in short, they spoke up and did not bump into the furniture.

Lucy Lorrimer was not a part with many opportunities; she is what the Hare-Grundy generation called an ingénue, a nice girl who feeds the birds ('They are God's creatures, and God gives the crumbs.')[30] and provides the incidental love interest. Her principal scene was with Hare himself, however, and offered her an object lesson in the triumph of an engaging stage presence over what even Hare acknowledged to be trite material.

A Pair of Spectacles ran only a month. This was partly a problem of box-office. Du Maurier's daughter Daphne observed a divide between 'the delight of those who remembered the original production and…the indifference of those who did not.'[31] The War had brought in new audiences, their factory or forces pay making theatre accessible despite an Entertainment Tax slapped on in 1916. If they wanted undemanding entertainment to lighten the Passchendaele autumn there was more life and spice at the everlasting *Chu Chin Chow* or *The Bing Boys*, where George Robey sang the most touching of all wartime love songs, 'If You Were the Only Girl in the World', or the revues that dominated the theatre of 1917 and brought ragtime to the West End.[32] If they wanted something more thoughtful, Ibsen's *Ghosts* and Brieux's *Damaged Goods* were playing to remind the responsible Tommy about the pitfalls of sexually transmitted disease. But younger playgoers had nothing to be nostalgic about and Victorian piety could not hold their attention.

There was also another reason to close: the air raids that were a feature of wartime London. This was the first time war had directly threatened civilians at home and it evoked very mixed responses in Londoners. There were no siren warnings, no procedures in place; people might huddle in the Tube, or stay where they were (even if that was on a tram) and turn out the lights, or they might go out and watch the raid as if it were a firework display – late-sitting MPs often did so. The policy of lighting the parks at night and leaving the streets in darkness to confuse bombers made theatre-going hazardous; those who could make the time preferred the new custom of matinee performances. In October 1915 two bombs narrowly missed the Strand Theatre, killing the callboy at the Gaiety and smashing a hole in the pavement as big as a double-decker bus. Fred Terry in his Scarlet Pimpernel silks gracefully defused incipient panic by leading the crowd in 'God Save the King'.

Late summer, 1917, saw another bomb dropped on the West End just as the theatres were emptying, and on the clear nights that punctuated the autumn storms enemy planes could be seen over the Thames in the beams of searchlights that swept the sky and guided the anti-aircraft guns. There was a moonlight raid only four nights into the run of *Spectacles*. Barrie invited Shaw, Hardy, Wells and Bennett onto the flat roof of his apartment in Adelphi Terrace to watch the explosions. Picking up fragments of shell the morning after, they concluded that English literature had narrowly avoided an irretrievable loss. Theatres might invite their patrons to leave the auditorium during a raid, but performances continued and most

---

[30] Sydney Grundy, *A Pair of Spectacles,* Nineteenth Century Plays ed. George Rowell (OUP1984), 528

[31] Daphne Du Maurier, *Gerald* (Penguin 1970), 143

[32] Gordon Williams, *British Theatre in the Great War* (Continuum 2000), 20

people chose to stay. Du Maurier inserted a note in the *Spectacles* programme: 'The whole of the auditorium at Wyndham's is covered by a main roof which consists of steel girders supporting two feet of concrete surrounded by asphalte [sic]'.

Hare's nerves, however, could not stand the strain and he went back into retirement, leaving Du Maurier to find a new play for Wyndham's. His choice, *Dear Brutus*, made sense for himself and for his theatre: Barrie was the most popular British dramatist and the role of Will Dearth fitted Du Maurier like a glove. However, it was to be a mixed blessing to Meggie, offered the female understudies. On the credit side, it was more than just a chance of work for a young actor glad of anything. It was an opportunity to work with an important stylistic innovator. Cedric Hardwicke, an early ADA pupil, recalled coming back from the Front to find that theatrical style seemed to have undergone a transformation. 'The resounding voices and broad gestures of my youth were frowned upon ...voices were dwindling to the conversational tones of front parlour gossip; gestures were diminishing to the flick of ash from a cigarette or the adjustment of shirt cuffs under a jacket. I had to start again....'[33]

The need for a more flexible and naturalistic style had become apparent since the English stage began to engage (privately, to evade the Lord Chamberlain) with Ibsen in the 1890s. The energies of pioneers like Barry Jackson and Annie Horniman pushed actors into a new strain of social realism. But the one responsible for bringing the more subtle style into the heart of the West End and popularizing it was Du Maurier. While he never spelt out any kind of theory of acting and adopted a deliberately flip tone when asked to do so, he had been evolving his technique since his days with Hare, and characteristically had his first triumph with a piece of dramatic fluff, *Raffles.* As the gentleman thief he held the stage for a long period in which he did not speak but allowed the dramatic force latent in his situation to do the work. His body made clear the subtext, the tension beneath the hero's casual high spirits. He made it look easy. Endless reviews that praised him but asserted that he was 'only playing himself'. Actors knew differently. Charles Laughton considered him the finest actor on the stage.

Du Maurier was one of the last actor-managers; unlike some, he believed in careful ensemble work rather than drilling fellow actors to stay out of his light. He took pains to teach his style, insofar as it could be taught:

> Don't force it, don't be self-conscious...Do what you generally do any day of your life when you come into a room. Bite your nails, yawn, lie down on a sofa and read a book – do anything or nothing, but don't look dramatically at the audience and speak with one eye on the right-hand box. If you must look in front of you, stare right at the back of the pit as though nobody was there.[34]

His technique as a director was to perform little parodies of the Victorian mannerisms some of his actors affected, followed by practical suggestions geared to helping them find their own way rather than copying à la Helen Haye.

While he had a protective, familial attitude to his casts, the playfulness was not just a way of energising rehearsal. It also established a way of assimilating and using older conventions. Barrie, Shaw and Wilde all used the structured climaxes,

---

[33] Cedric Hardwicke, *A Victorian in Orbit,* (Methuen 1961), 102
[34] Daphne Du Maurier, *Gerald,* 119

the set responses of Victorian carriage-trade dramas, but placed them in a context that undercut the attitudes behind them. Du Maurier, who had created the role of Mr Darling/Captain Hook, knew the dramatic value of heroic poses and climactic addresses to the right hand box, but he was also aware that they indicated hollowness rather than nobility; he postured to encourage the audience to view a character with a cynical eye. He preferred to show true love through a casual hug or a rude epithet in a bantering tone.

This was a style that would radically shape the drama of the twenties. Without the Du Maurier style – flippant surface masking underlying pain – there would be no one to perform the work of Coward, for example. As training for the role of the tragic Sydney in *A Bill Of Divorcement* a season with Du Maurier could not be bettered.

Will Dearth, bitter, alcoholic and shackled to a wife who despises him, is one of the few characters in *Dear Brutus* who does not deceive himself and does not strike Victorian attitudes about love and fidelity. When everyone enters the magic wood where their alternative lives are revealed, he is transformed into the playful and loving father of a daughter who only exists in his dreams. The role stretched him as few others and to work with him was an education.

Du Maurier liked to think he had discovered Meggie. He thought highly of her work in *Spectacles.* He was grateful for her cheerfulness during the worst raids; the stress that older cast members experienced was mitigated by the presence of someone too young to fear for herself. He was keen to offer her something; *Dear Brutus* was the best play of the year and the presence of Barrie, who valued rehearsal over performance and could offer trenchant advice, was an added bonus. But there was no role in *Dear Brutus* for which she could be properly cast. Barrie always had clear images of his characters, and his stage directions make it clear that what he wanted from Margaret, the dream child, was a physicality on the edge of adolescence: '*She is all legs.... she has as many freckles as there are stars in heaven. She is as lovely as you think she is, and she is aged the moment when you like your daughter best.*'

His first impulse was to offer the part to Cynthia Asquith, whose pre-Raphaelite beauty owed nothing to contemporary fashion; but she had no interest in acting and opted to become his secretary. The role went to Faith Celli, just sixteen, with a face like a Renaissance angel. Emlyn Williams, a smitten undergraduate, wrote, 'I would stare at her in disbelief and thought, if I saw her walking along [the] High Street. I would kneel and expect the rest to follow suit.'[35] Her notices were brilliant, a tribute not simply to her own talent but to a cast who bonded over the creation of the play into an organic unit and made it difficult to visualise a better alternative.

Meggie had the emotional range for Margaret, but she was short, stocky and dark. She didn't waft. She looked real, and the magic of the play lay precisely in the fragile half-life of the dream child at a point in history when nobody could take the lives of their children for granted. Even Effie preferred Celli, who was in any case disgustingly healthy, and Meggie played the role only once. Her luck was not much better with her other understudy as Joanna Trout. This was even worse casting. Barrie might give twee stage directions about freckles and stars, but his analysis of sexual politics was the most mordant of his generation. Joanna is a sentimental, self-deceiving and faithless airhead, and gets precisely the man she deserves. Meggie

[35] Emlyn Williams, *George* (Reprint Society 1962), 278

looked far too young for the role and lacked the experience to develop its acidic comedy. The opportunity only occurred once anyway.

It must have been, to some extent, a relief, in that she could have had no illusions about her suitability for the roles. This was her longest period without any opportunity to perform; although in later years she experienced illness and emotional stress it is the only time when she seems to have been seriously withdrawn. The brief sketch of her by Du Maurier as 'wistful and alone, which was always my impression of her'[36], does not accord with many people's recollections. It is as if the fact of being able to perform coloured the whole of her world.

This perhaps explains why she made a mess of her first encounter with Basil Dean; as he remembered it, 'She was listless and full of complaint against Gerald Du Maurier for not giving her a chance to act.'[37] If his memory is correct, they met during the run of *Brutus,* which ended before Dean was in a position to offer her anything, so there would have been no question of an audition. This might have pushed her frustration into rudeness. Coming from an actress a year out of drama school, even one working with a reputable manager and associated with a good production, her complaints sounded like arrogance.

The only work she was to have during the run of *Brutus* seems to have been an appearance in one of the Endell Street Hospital pantomimes for wounded soldiers, organised by Alix Grein, wife of J.T. Grein, founder of the Independent Theatre, successful in her own right as a dramatist under the name Michael Orme. She recalled Meggie as 'the sweetest Cinderella imaginable'[38] among a distinguished cast which included the lugubriously camp Ernest Thesiger as a ballerina, his dress modelled – as in life – on that of Queen Mary. The more gravely disfigured soldiers in the audience were discreetly hidden behind screens.

The War, however, could not be shut out. Eva had given up the Slade to become a VAD. Effie threw regular Sunday evenings for young soldiers in town, many of them the sons of her own friends, who in the dance-crazy era would roll back the carpets and dance to ragtime. Not all of them came back, including the son of James Douglas. Effie recalled that on one Sunday, three of the guests who returned to France next morning were killed by the end of the week. Some did come back, but profoundly damaged. Marshall Curtis Brown, Meggie and Eva's childhood friend, was gassed; the only treatment for the ruined lungs was morphine; like many soldiers he found the withdrawal process agonising and never fully recovered. His marriage to Eva was to be brief and painful. At Wyndham's, Du Maurier, tormented by the death of his brother in action, abandoned what could have been a long and successful run and joined up at the age of forty-five; too impatient to negotiate a commission, he went as a private soldier.

Meanwhile Effie was approached by her friend Julia Neilson, who asked if she would be willing to let Meggie tour with the Neilson-Terry company in *Henry of Navarre.* Effie had no problem persuading Wyndham's to release an understudy from a play that would clearly not run much longer. The new project suited everybody: Meggie had been an ardent Fred Terry fan since her childhood; Effie, perhaps mindful of Du Maurier's reputation as a womaniser, decided with parental optimism that Julia would be a 'magnificent moral influence'.[39]

---

[36] *Meggie Albanesi,* 58

[37] Basil Dean, *Seven Ages,* (Hutchinson 1970), 139

[38] Michael Orme, *J.T.Grein* (John Murray 1936), 200

[39] *Meggie Albanesi,* 54

The husband-and-wife team were certainly pillars of Victorian respectability. Fred disapproved of his elder sister, Ellen Terry, for her more free and easy attitude to sex. He detested the New Drama and despised Oscar Wilde and his 'unhealthy' wit. Until the war had parted them he had corrosive political arguments with his son Dennis, who did brilliant and more up-to-date work for Granville Barker – arguments Fred invariably lost which left him seething with anti-intellectualism. But the hoped-for 'moral influence' of the Terrys could perhaps be seen at its best in management terms. Touring could be lonely and lodgings sleazy; young actresses found themselves very vulnerable. The Terrys combined a real interest in the welfare of their employees ('Terry's lambs', they called them) with a love of luxury that made touring necessary in the first place. They followed the custom of the grandest actor-managers of the 1890s and had their own train, with the names of the cast in large type pasted onto the windows.

The First Company on the Road, as they were known, had an unspoken right to the best available lodgings in every town. The Terrys ensured that there was always enough to eat during the long Sunday wait to change trains at Crewe and threw cast parties at the end of every run. If they did not pay the highest salaries in the profession, they never sacked anybody: the company grew larger and larger; and as the war ground on they were increasingly solicitous for its younger members, mindful of Dennis at the front.

Neilson and Terry knew what they had to offer the public and it wasn't the New Drama. *Henry of Navarre,* like *The Scarlet Pimpernel*, was tosh; but they had successfully played it for a decade because it was *their* tosh. Fred was inventive with stage business and a master at controlling atmosphere in the auditorium; he could transform a script to fit him like his own skin (some of his amendments are fossilised in the novel of *Pimpernel,* incorporated by the author who recognised that he had developed the character). As Max Beerbohm put it, 'The public demands that Mr Terry shall be a devil of a fellow...Miss Neilson is famous for flouncing and bouncing contemptuously round the stage, tossing her head and covering suitors with raillery...the proud set face that masks the breaking heart of beauty neglected is a thing which the public has a right to demand for a few minutes every evening.'[40] Hence there were sword fights; disguises, pavanes, ghosts, low comedy, gorgeous costumes and an opportunity for Fred to assume a variety of accents, in a plot so convoluted nobody had time to reflect how silly it was.

Fred was the youngest child of Ben Terry, who began his career in the 1840s; his idol, apprehended through stories rather than experience, was Edmund Kean. It was this Romantic, flashes-of-lightning tradition to which Fred aspired; his own role model was Henry Irving. While Du Maurier and his imitators treated the Irving style with affectionate mockery, Fred was one of the few who could still make it work. He was now plump, suffering from gout, short sight and weak heart; but he remained one of the most attractive of a handsome family and he still had the fire and magic to make his swashbuckling prince convincing. While Julia's work could be patchy, her talent for tragic melodrama rather than the usual Terry tosh, Fred's soubriquet 'the Golden Terry' went on being quoted in reviews without irony and never fell into disuse. John Gielgud, sceptical about the talents of some of his Terry family, preferred Fred's panache to Du Maurier's naturalism and considered him a great actor.

Terry did not have a technical vocabulary, but in rehearsal he had both

---

[40] Beerbohm, *Last Theatres,* 425

patience and the experience to suggest ideas that helped a timid performer to fit into the machinery of the play; if he was limited in his tastes, his own dramatic vehicles never bored him. For him, they remained genuinely exciting, the suspense of the battles and the sex-appeal of the courtly love scenes were minted new every time, and he could transmit this zest to his company. The younger members considered themselves as students:

> One of the good things in the Company was that the new or young members were not only allowed but also encouraged to stand in the wings; in some of the smaller provincial theatres this led us into trouble with the Stage Manager, but we became skilful in dodging him, in suspending ourselves from ladders or flattening ourselves up in the flies. And not only the small-fry but also the principals often crowded the wings to see the Chief's first act, from which we learned far more of our business as actors than we gained from half a dozen rehearsals.[41]

The tour offered an opportunity to see a craftsman fine-tuning a role; every night there were minute variations, geared to another theatre, another audience. Because the play was so much Fred Terry's, it was possible to see him engaging with each new encounter, the careful manipulation of his personal charisma. For a new performer, too, there was the chance to explore different theatres, to put the training to the test and adjust the voice and the body in new spaces. Meggie was always to remain grateful to the Terrys for giving her the solid experience she needed to back up her ambition.

If the tour had a risk, it was that one could become stuck in the Terry style. Fred was one of the last actor-managers to use the labels once employed by all stock companies like his father's: leading man, leading lady, heavy man, first low comedian, leading juvenile woman, first chambermaid, second walking lady and utility. The hierarchy they implied both defined company structure and created the world of their plays. A talented performer could rise through the ranks, but also absorbed a way of defining the self on stage that could become a class-bound carapace, 'leading juvenile woman' rather than a complex individual. Fred's acting persona was his own; rather than making himself look dated by awkward experiment (as his swashbuckling rival Lewis Waller did) he opted to retain the integrity of his style. However, young 'Terry lambs' could be seen as mannered, unsuited to modern dress and techniques.

Meggie left after four months; her health was a trouble, and she needed an operation on a wisdom tooth, but it was a good time to move on. What she had gained, apart from a confidence born of coping with audiences all over the country and the discipline of a long run, was Terry panache to balance Du Maurier restraint. Du Maurier felt that a role like Richard III was off limits because his regular audience would find it 'embarrassing'.[42] The vibrant physicality of the Terry style could always be modified, but those of the new generation who had not had the chance to express themselves through body as well as text could find themselves disempowered. Teaching at the now-Royal Academy of Dramatic Art in 1922, Sybil Thorndike picked out John Gielgud as the only student with 'guts', complaining that

---

[41] Marguerite Steen, *A Pride of Terrys* (Longmans 1962), 287
[42] Sheridan Morley, *John Gielgud,* (Hodder and Stoughton 2001), 49

the rest 'were all trying to be Gerald Du Maurier and that's no way to approach Greek tragedy.'[43]

As an actress who wanted real range and classic roles, Meggie had the great advantage of encountering one of the last great Victorians and the most elegant Edwardian; whatever the dying art of the actor-manager could give, she had seized with both hands.

---

[43] Morley, *John Gielgud*, 34

'Roots beneath the water'

1919

Throughout 1919, *The Times* published lists of the newly identified dead; grief remained raw for thousands. Returning soldiers found nobody at home to listen to their experiences – nor, Wilfred Owen suggested, were they fit to speak of them. There were endless reminders of the past, from advertisements proclaiming the virtues of Cailler's Cocoa, 'one of Tommy's greatest comforts while in the Trenches' to the solemn arrival home of the celebrated dead, such as Edith Cavell, and the first two-minute silence in November.

Fred Terry spoke at the annual Theatrical Fund Festival at the Savoy, the first since the War began. He indicated that the days ahead might be difficult for actors. Lilian Braithwaite replied on behalf of the Actors Association. Aware that Terry was right about prospects, but wanting more than charity, the profession began to unionise itself a week after the Armistice, demanding a standard contract of employment and pushing for rehearsal pay, Unemployment was rising, and continued to rise as jobs and homes for returning heroes failed to materialise.

In the theatre, old structures were breaking up. The actor-managers had largely been bought out, and a new attitude to theatre and commerce emerged. While Irving and the rest might be conservative and egocentric in their tastes, profits were ploughed back into their companies, not given to shareholders. If a play failed, they could at least interpret the mood of the audience at first hand and respond swiftly. The new impresarios were reluctant to take chances. Critics complained of 'fluff' during the war years, but this was a function of safety-first management rather than audience taste,[44] and showed little sign of changing. Backers favoured the star system over ensemble acting; it was cheaper in the end to pay out £80 a week for a well-known face and cut the salaries of the lesser lights. And as Cedric Hardwicke bitterly remarked, it paid the new middlemen to buy up and re-let theatre leases 'like penny socks'[45]: the lease of one theatre rose from £20 to £500 a week in months. The resulting inflation had repercussions throughout the theatre world. In this climate playhouses lacked coherent policies or individual traditions, so a revue might follow hard on the heels of Ibsen or Shaw.

Cicely Hamilton pointed out that a theatre '[stood] no more chance of attaining the distinction of personality than…a democratic State which disposed of its rulers at every successive election.'[46] If the stately Toryism of Irving was threatened there was also a gap left by the radicals who brought Ibsen to the country at the close of the nineteenth century and created the Vedrenne-Barker partnership at the Royal Court between 1904 and 1907. The writers they had championed,

---

[44] See Gordon Williams, *British Theatre in the Great War* (Continuum 2003), 151

[45] Hardwicke, *A Victorian in Orbit*, 98

[46] Quoted by James Agate, *A Short View of the English Stage(* Herbert Jenkins 1926), 29

Shaw, Barker, Galsworthy, were still working, but their successors had not yet been found and no one seemed to be looking.

Meggie's picture appeared in a 1919 *Tatler* as 'one of the coming stage debutantes of the New Year', the article inexplicably conflating her parents into 'the world-famous actress and prima donna Madame Albanesi'.[47] Her first engagement might have suited the society girl suggested by this bit of publicity. C.B.Cochran was one of the most powerful managers of his era. His taste ran from Ibsen to flea circuses; his sophisticated revues brought a touch of Paris to wartime entertainment and his first nights were social occasions to rival a debutantes' ball – with some of the debutantes onstage. He was currently mounting a revival of *Cyrano de Bergerac*. It was an astute bid to set the post-war tone for the commercial theatre, combining elegiac laments for fallen heroes with spectacle to rival *Chu Chin Chow*. There were sets and costumes by Edmond Dulac in his vivid enamelled style. Roxane was Mrs Patrick Campbell, no longer young but her starry reputation undimmed. Cyrano was Robert Loraine, an accomplished actor whose status as returning war hero was shrewdly exploited; as the *Sketch* put it, 'Cyrano: Late RAF: Arras Trenches: A New Nose.' As often with Cochran, rehearsals were long and exhausting while he marshalled scores of extras. The show opened in March at the Garrick, moving to the more majestic Drury Lane in May.

While a society girl might walk on as a nun, as Meggie did in the last act, there was a stronger part for her after her touring experience. Lise, the baker's wife, is a snappy flirt no better than she should be. The role is small but prominent, the protagonist's first real encounter with a woman; it allows the performer to place a funny line, to create a chemistry with the leading actor, to display the individuality of her comic talent. This was the first part to let Meggie show herself as an artist rather than a sweet stage presence, a chance to establish to a substantial public the kind of actress that she would be.

During *Cyrano* Meggie had her first encounter with one of the woman mentors who were to enrich her career. The real vitality of British theatre at this point depended less on the West End than on 'other' theatres whose priorities were not primarily commercial. Annie Horniman's brilliant repertory theatre in Manchester had collapsed in 1919, but its descendants in Birmingham and Liverpool offered innovative interpretations of the classics and new plays with a political edge. The Old Vic was providing Shakespeare on a shoestring. Subscription clubs, like Grein's Independent Theatre, the Stage Society, the Phoenix Society, the 300 Club and the Pioneer Players had always been alive to new work by both British and European playwrights. Many societies, like the Pioneers, had no settled home, but subscriptions mounted Sunday (and sometimes Monday afternoon) performances in venues such as the Kingsway or the Ambassadors three or four times a year.

A character in *The Rising Sun,* the play that launched Meggie as a star, belongs to just such an organisation and wryly describes its relationship with the critics:

> When we give tragedy they ask why we don't do clean
> wholesome plays with a happy ending, and when we take their advice
> they complain that we are not justifying our existence.

---

[47] *Tatler*, 22 June 1919

> When we do a classic they say we ought to patronise unknown dramatists, but if we produce a new play they encourage us by refusing to find any merit in it.[48]

Edith Craig, the founder of the Pioneer Players, was a veteran of such arguments. The Pioneers, one of the few Edwardian stage societies to survive the War, had grown out of the Actresses' Franchise League and produced a remarkable range of work associated with feminist issues. Their policy, however, was simply to stage plays 'which may be outside the province of the commercial theatre, as at present constituted, yet none the less sincere manifestations of the dramatic spirit'.[49] They explored naturalist, expressionist and symbolist theatre. Edith Craig's notions of *mise-en-scène* influenced and were influenced by those of her brother Edward Gordon Craig. They actively sought plays from other countries (even during the War, a controversial stance) and made their own translations when necessary. Their members saw a broader spectrum of theatre than that offered by wealthier organisations, and their productions were reviewed in Europe as well as in England.

The Pioneers provided a supportive context for a young performer. Because productions were limited to one or two performances, they broke down distinctions between the experienced and the novice, amateur and professional. Leading performers worked with them because they shared their values and welcomed the refreshment during long West End runs; newer presences, such as Sybil Thorndike, considered their careers to have been substantially advanced by the Pioneers.[50] The working atmosphere was stimulating – especially to women, who despite the eclecticism of society policy were given unrivalled opportunities in most fields of theatrical work. Craig in particular could devise extraordinary effects on a minimal budget, a process that involved her dragging anyone able and available into every aspect of the work from walking on to devising props.

Although the Pioneers were not a company as such, the consistent work of Craig's partners, the painter Clare Atwood and the writer Christopher St John, and the continuing support of the membership, developed a kind of company spirit at a time when ensemble work was not universally valued. Craig was a charismatic director – Thorndike compared her to Granville Barker. 'To me, it was like seeing the Da Vinci hands for the first time, or a chord of Bach – putting me in a place where I was able to grasp and convey the meaning myself.'[51] Miss La Trobe in Virginia Woolf's *Between the Acts* is a thinly disguised portrait of Craig: an eccentric, inventive figure never satisfied with her own efforts but with an instinct for empowering her players and unearthing the energies that will give them personal success in a role, what Woolf called 'the roots beneath the water'.[52]

In Meggie Craig discerned the power to carry the movement of a complex play on her shoulders despite her inexperience. *The Rising Sun* is a socialist-realist drama by the Dutch writer Herman Heijermans, equally noted for the slashing power of his reportage and criticism. It deals with the impact of a big store, the 'Sun', on a family of small shopkeepers. There is explicit political confrontation, as well as telling incidental sideswipes at anti-Semitism and the timidity of commercial

---

[48] Herman Heijermans, *The Rising Sun,* tr. Christopher St John (Labour Publishing Co. 1925), 34

[49] Fifth Annual Report of the society cited in V. Gardner and S. Rutherford, *The New Woman and her Sisters,* (Harvester Wheatsheaf 1992), 233

[50] Katherine Cockin , *Women and Theatre in the Age of Suffrage*, 13

[51] Eleanor Adlard (ed) *Edy: Recollections of Edith Craig* (Frederick Muller 1949), 79

[52] Virginia Woolf, *Between the Acts,* (Hogarth Press 1941), 80

theatre; but the play is also the personal tragedy of the young girl Sonia. Aware that insurance may provide a way out, she allows herself to drop a lamp and start a fire which kills the handicapped child of the woman in the upstairs flat; her remorse brings her to the edge of madness until her father, refusing to profit by the situation, leads her to confess to arson.

Christopher St John writes in the preface to her translation that the text is difficult to read because of its 'dramatic shorthand'.[53] Heijermans avoids spelling out the issues; the play demands attention to subtext in every facet of the production. The economic impact of the store is shown through lighting, the neon radiance of the Rising Sun set against the half-lit chandeliers and faulty lamps of the small establishment. The emotional consequence, the alliance between Sonia, her father Matthew and her young man Nat in the face of pressure by weaker members of the family to sell up, is expressed through jokes and allusions and casual gestures of affection. The play combined Craig's own socialist politics with the opportunity for sophisticated lighting and set achieved on a shoestring.

Sonia is the most complex role in the play. The audience sees the action from her point of view, and she is rarely offstage. Her emotional journey provides the throughline of the plot and can easily turn to melodrama. It is possible to extract what Victorian actors called 'points' – striking moments in the revelation of character or situation emphasised by a special gesture or tone of voice. (Twenty years previously Shaw was complaining about English Ibsen on that score.[54]) Meggie and Leon Quartermaine avoided 'points' in favour of subtext. Quartermaine's voice was dry and academic and did not lend itself to sentiment; they let the strength of the father-daughter relationship, on which the credibility of the ending depends, establish itself through the comedy and cross-talk with which the text gives it a footing in reality.

Sonia also carries the most overtly political scene in the play; she is alone when Jensen, the owner of the Rising Sun, turns up. Like Shaw, Heijermans allows his capitalist some dignity; the scene is not black and white and demands a clear understanding by the performers of the issues at stake. Jensen does not take advantage of the fact that Sonia has signed a bill although she is under age, pointing out that he does not need to be underhand. 'It's merely a question of power.'[55] While his calm sets the overall tone, the fine tuning of the scene has to be controlled by the actor playing Sonia; she is the one who has to conceal her emotions and this is what sustains the tension of their verbal duel. Throughout, Sonia is performing domestic tasks – waiting on her complaining mother in the next room, cooking for her father; she is also furtively ringing the bell to the shop to give the impression that they still have customers, and keeping an eye on Jensen who is looking for an opportunity to peek at the books. The actions are not just 'business' but a silent language through which Sonia needs to make clear her concern for the family, her defiance - and her fear - of Jensen, and the sometimes comical immaturity of her tactics; only at the end is she allowed an overt outburst of rage against 'your low prices, your big plate glass windows, your advertisements, your glaring lights'.[56]

When the emotional stress of this confrontation gives way to another kind, as her father and his friends erupt into the room for a celebration they can't afford,

---

[53] Christopher St John, Introduction to *The Rising Sun*, vi

[54] *Saturday Review,* 15 May 1897

[55] *The Rising Sun*, 58

[56] *The Rising Sun*, 57

the playwright gives the actress an opportunity to think her way through to the crisis of the role. The audience sees Sonia leaving to fetch the lamp; every material detail that could allow her action to be an accident, including the icy patch on the floor, is as carefully planted as the sources of her very mixed feelings. The actress may or may not choose to give the audience an indication of Sonia's motivation; she may allow the decision to be made later, when she is offstage, she may choose to show whether she feels tempted to the arson she finally commits. The text trusts the performer to respond imaginatively to both the emotional situation and the physical space.

The final act is profoundly testing; Sonia is on the verge of breakdown, like Nina at the end of *The Seagull.* The text does more than put her at the emotional centre of the scene; waking nightmares reveals her mental state, so that through Sonia the audience sees what has never been directly shown, the death of the child. The text concentrates on domestic details – Sonia's attempts to tidy the ruined house, the way Nat cares for her, pulling from her frozen feet the shoes that she has worn for days, ready for the arrival of the police. These create anchors for naturalistic performance, so that the world of Sonia and her father remains believable while they undergo their last struggle to act according to their own ethical code.

The play was staged on 1 June at the Lyric, Hammersmith. Nigel Playfair had only recently rescued this beautiful theatre from decay; it was known as 'the blood and flea pit' and the dressing rooms still lived up to the name. The successful run of *Abraham Lincoln* throughout 1919 was the start of Playfair's thirteen-year tenure, which would establish it as one of the most interesting venues in London. The Lyric's drawing power was already something from which Edith Craig and the Pioneers could benefit and *The Rising Sun* sold well. The response was all Craig could wish for. *The Times* recorded that 'not many private theatrical performances on Sunday afternoons end in scenes of enthusiasm'[57] and praised the naturalistic intimacy achieved in the father-daughter relationship and the spiritual power that shone through it: 'Miss Albanesi's acting moved us profoundly by its passion and charmed us wholly with its beauty.'

The cast were also lavish in their praise. Meggie received nine curtain calls and Craig presented her to her mother Ellen Terry; her own career almost at its close – although she was still playing Juliet's nurse – Terry encouraged her as she did other exceptional new players of this fertile period, including Edith Evans and John Gielgud. Meggie, however, would die before Terry.

Christopher St John dedicated her published translation of the play 'to Meggie, whose talent first burst into flower in the part of Sonia'. This is a just claim; despite her ADA successes it was this play, and the Pioneers, that allowed her to discover her 'roots beneath the water'. St John's assessment of Meggie after her death is one of the most insightful; she suggests that the quality that drew Craig to cast her in *The Rising Sun* was that of honesty. 'She expressed herself...in primary colours, with a frankness and cleanness that made every character she impersonated seem amazingly simple.'[58]

'Simple' might sound paradoxical applied to a character like Sonia, whose multiple facets St John had struggled to express in her translation; she uses it here not to indicate a reduction of complex characters to one-dimensional figures like

---

[57] *The Times*, 2 June 1919

[58] *Time and Tide*, 18 Jan 1924

Lucy in *Spectacles*, but the clarity with which, moment by moment, they need to be revealed. The actor who offers the audience this simplicity does so by sharing with them the quality of her attention, focused precisely on what the character does and sees. Declan Donnellan suggests that the ability to 'act' is essentially our innate ability to learn by copying and imitating others, the most elementary of our survival tools, and that bad 'acting' in the theatrical sense indicates the inhibition of that natural state. 'Rather than claim that x is more talented than y it is more accurate to say that x is less blocked than y. The talent is already pumping away, like the circulation of the blood.'[59] There was nothing to stand in the way of Meggie Albanesi's performance, no overt demands for sympathy for the character, nothing artificially imposed in the way of illustration or decoration: she simply gave it. The contribution of Craig and the Pioneers was to offer her a context in which this process was supported and in which the outcome mattered because theatre itself mattered – where the act of performance could legitimately engage the whole person, politically, emotionally and spiritually.

Meanwhile there were bread and butter opportunities; she worked in several films. None were more than hastily shot versions of popular stage hits, but she did graduate from glorified walk-ons in *Darby and Joan* and the euphoniously titled *Better 'Ole* to playing a vamp in *A Great Day* and Matheson Lang's daughter, Nang Ping, in *Mr Wu*; she enjoyed the outdoor location work, and took to Lang, an actor in the Terry grand manner, who later introduced her to Victor Sjöstrom and a more ambitious kind of filming. She felt that she was 'no earthly' on film. She liked to revise and develop a role rather than see 'some little false move' permanently captured on celluloid.[60]

She did impress another of the *Mr Wu* cast, Lillah McCarthy. This meant that during preparations for *The Rising Sun* she was already in rehearsal for another play with a dynamic woman director, like Craig a veteran of the Actresses' Franchise League. McCarthy had played Helena in Granville-Barker's groundbreaking *A Midsummer Night's Dream* with its stress on fast and simple staging and perfect verse speaking. She had been one of the key players of the Vedrenne-Barker period at the Court, and Shaw claimed she had inspired the role of Ann Whitfield in *Man and Superman*. He valued the way she transposed the style she learned barnstorming around the world in Wilson Barrett's *The Sign of the Cross* onto political drama, asserting that her 'secret was that she combined the executive art of the grand school with a natural impulse to murder the Victorian womanly woman.'[61]

After a painful divorce from Granville-Barker and a war spent organizing high-powered charity events McCarthy decided that she wanted to manage her own company and perform with it. She raised five thousand pounds from friends and persuaded Arnold Bennett to write *Judith*. It was a disaster. With half the money gone, she looked for something 'simple, amusing, well-constructed'[62] to rescue herself and plumped for Eden Phillpotts's *St George and the Dragons*, moderately successful at Birmingham the previous year. Her cast she considered 'brilliant' and the attractive playhouse, the Kingsway, had been restyled and launched by one of the pioneers of female management, Lena Ashwell. The only problem was the script.

[59] Declan Donnellan, *The Actor and the Target* (NHB 2002), 6
[60] Interview with May Herschel Clarke, 21 Aug 1920, Mander and Mitchenson file on Albanesi
[61] Shaw, Preface to Lillah McCarthy, *Myself and My Friends,*(Thornton Butterworth 1933), 8
[62] McCarthy, *Myself and My Friends,* 31

As the four-year London run of Barry Jackson's Birmingham production *The Farmer's Wife* proved, Phillpotts could write with wit and warmth but *George* leaves a slightly unpleasant taste in the mouth. It's the story of a bishop's intrigues to prevent his daughters marrying 'beneath' them. Monica has a Lawrentian yen for a farm labourer and is duly exposed to the reality of country life (including seeing her suitor drunk). Eva fancies a curate only to see him lured by a prestigious chaplaincy conditional on his celibacy. The bishop has the best lines; played by Ernest Thesiger as the campest cleric outside the novels of Ronald Firbank, he evolved a relationship with the audience that had both warmth and sophistication. The roles of the daughters have almost nothing to offer. They satirise the 'flapper', a standard target of the period, but, as J.T. Grein complained, the language was inadequate, 'amazingly lacking in the colloquialisms which are as current in our country houses as in our public schools'.[63]

McCarthy did a rescue job by developing a double act with Meggie. Her instinct for Shavian parody of the grand style chimed with what Meggie had learned from Du Maurier; they evolved symmetrical gestures that turned the silly girls into mirror images, Meggie as the curate-fancier aping the rhythms and gestures of McCarthy's rustic free spirit. Stressing rather than concealing the artificiality of the characters at least kept the comedy on the boil, and *The Times* recognised the skill involved. 'We fear that the revolting daughters are only inventions, though it must be added that they are sufficiently diverting inventions as presented by Miss McCarthy and Miss Meggie Albanesi.'[64] Despite much goodwill towards McCarthy (not to mention block bookings by the Devonshire and Somerset Regiments supporting a West Country drama) the play was a box office failure. 'St George,' lamented McCarthy, 'who had never failed England, failed me.'[65] But she had passed on to Meggie some of her experience of the Court tradition. The play also brought Meggie to the notice of Clemence Dane, who saw in her comic skills something of value for *A Bill of Divorcement.* Meanwhile, the failure of *George* left her depressed; she was always to blame herself when a play did not work, however strong her own contribution.

The next opportunity came within weeks, the role of Sasha in Tolstoy's *The Living Corpse,* (wisely retitled *Reparation*), the vehicle Henry Ainley had chosen to celebrate his belated demobilisation. Going into management with Gilbert Miller, he mounted a lavish production which toured the north of England for a month before arriving at the St James's Theatre in September. Ainley was a genius, if an erratic one. He was considered to have the most beautiful voice on the English stage, his panache and energy could carry a production and his good looks won him the label 'idol' from the press. He also drank. In rehearsal he could lapse into an uncommunicative haze, marking rather than performing, then suddenly flashing into brilliance for long enough to get the applause of his fellow actors.

His role, a rake who realises that his wife and family are better off without him and fakes his own death, spoke to Ainley's own condition; he had a brilliant cast, including Marion Terry (in Gielgud's opinion, the best of all the acting Terrys), Athene Seyler and Claude Rains in dapper comic mode. It was a bold choice of play that tapped into a developing interest in all things Russian; despite a distrust of 'Bolshevism' that characterised the next few decades, translations of Russian novels

---

[63] *Illustrated London News*, 21 June 1919
[64] *The Times*, 12 June 1919
[65] McCarthy, *Myself and My Friends,* 31

and plays followed hard upon the interest roused by the Russian Ballet. Ainley promoted it with enthusiasm, giving interviews in the press to explain how to pronounce Russian names.

Special performances were organised by the Russian Musical Dramatic Art Society (ДФРВФ) whose fortnightly events aimed 'to unite all friends of Russia and Russians by a better understanding of her soul – expressed in her art'. One evening comprised a massive bill that began with music at 5.30 and also included a full-length ballet with Karsarvina as well as *Reparation*. Later there was a matinee for the Russian Red Cross, patronised by a horde of English and Russian royalty. A moving force on the ДФРВФ council included Komisarjevsky, who had fled the regime in 1920 after running both the Imperial and the State Theatres in Moscow; he became one of the leading directors in Britain, setting the style for English Chekhov. As a first step towards a new post-war theatre Ainley's move could not have been timelier and the contact with Komisarjevsky was invaluable for his cast. Meggie's role was that of the young sister-in-law who comes closest to understanding the disreputable Fedya. They have only one scene together, but as a critic remembered four years afterwards, 'in her hands it became the pivot of the play, the actual manifestation of the author's meaning.'[66] It is likely both actors identified this scene as the moral centre of the play; it is the only one in which the dissolute hero is engaged in something resembling an equal conversation. Most of Fedya's scenes involve people reacting to his behaviour. He and Sasha are interested in each other, refreshing for the actor and the audience. Her plea to him to stay is a principled one but born of her desire to cling to the image of a loving family; he gently explains to her how marriages can go irreparably wrong.

The scene floats gently on an unspoken thought: Sasha's constant defence of Fedya while the family erupt around her suggests she is in love with him without knowing it. His gentleness to her suggests that he knows, but will not disturb her innocence. The subtext allows the audience to develop a relationship with the characters subconsciously rather than sitting in judgement; it guarantees the reality of figures that might otherwise remain personified issues.

Ainley and Meggie were well contrasted, their looks running counter to the way a conventional production might cast them: Ainley's aristocratic profile shone through his seedy beard and poor skin tone. Meggie's stocky peasant earthiness undercut any attempt to make Sasha angelic; her photograph shows her focused and intent, her gaze steady but not offering any kind of reproach – the look of someone who sees the person they are addressing, not a list of their good or bad actions. Vocally too they were cast against type. Ainley had one of those golden voices that make speech sound like music; hers was, as Christopher St John described it, full of 'rough dark tones, which move the listener more than insipid sweet ones'.[67]

The sets realistically showed the varied social backgrounds of the play; they were based on designs from the original Moscow Arts production. *Reparation* was one of the earliest British attempts to engage with some of its innovations. The opportunity to pioneer Chekhov would arrive in time for the young Gielgud and Ashcroft to take full advantage of it. This was to be Meggie's only encounter with Russian theatre, in a play Tolstoy had never really finished and refused to allow onstage in his own lifetime. It offered moments of genuine power with some

---

[66] Cecil Chesterton, *The Sphere,* 22 Dec 1923

[67] *Time and Tide*, 18 Jan 1924

wooden characterisation and a plot not completely worked out. The *Tatler* complained of the 'silly' people but praised its 'dramatic and intellectual grip'.[68]

Reparation was a critical success despite a rail strike which did not help the houses. During the run Meggie went for a second interview with Basil Dean, whose plans for a new company were on their way and who was anxious for her to become a member. But she was still smouldering from their last encounter and this time Dean seems to have been the one to mess up the meeting. 'I thought her conceited, and said so. She thought me too managerial and unapproachable; I suppose I was. It was all very foolish, and the interview terminated abruptly.'[69] She may have felt unwilling to commit herself to a venture whose aims were not yet clear to her; nor would she be the first person to dislike the often-abrasive Dean on sight. This time, too, she was really working, not an understudy, and there were some interesting roles with established theatre societies in prospect to vary the pace.

In October the Incorporated Stage Society put on two performances of Herbert Trench's *Napoleon* to celebrate its twenty-first season. With a cast of twenty-eight, eleven discursive scenes in blank verse including a closely structured debate between Napoleon and a pacifist mapmaker, and action sequences which, the *Telegraph* suggested, 'would have seemed a trifle daring to d'Artagnan'[70] it was not a commercial proposition and only a subscription society would mount it. However, it was attractive to actors. The play reunited Meggie with Edith Craig and Leon Quartermaine from *The Rising Sun* and her old ADA tutor A.E. George, playing Napoleon.

It also introduced her to an actress who would become a kind friend, Sybil Thorndike. For some of the cast the attraction lay in the heroic verse: Thorndike had a saintly role in contrast with her recent excursions into Greek tragedy and for many the image of her quietly rocking the cloak of her dead son was worth the price of admission. For Meggie, it was an opportunity to give a fully developed comic performance. Her role as Thorndike's French actress niece had nothing to do with the action of the play. But it provided the only laughter in a sea of blank verse; her character flirts with Napoleon and he struggles to preserve his icy public image while trying to nail her address. It was the most self-assured character she had played, with consequent risks attached: if Elise's sparkle does not dominate the stage she is an embarrassment rather than much-needed comic relief.

In the event the critical honours were divided between Thorndike and Albanesi; there was widespread acknowledgement that despite the play's vagaries she had made a step forward. While she had always been noted for emotional intensity, she was now seen to possess authority. 'How fast she is learning the self-conduct, the technique of acting, so that she can play a finished little woman of the world without losing a touch of that finished little person's humanity,'[71] wrote St John Ervine. Such a response made it clear that *The Rising Sun* was not a lucky coincidence of actress and script at the right moment. It also reveals her as a performer who was being watched with care and would increasingly be judged against her own achieved standards.

The year closed with another Stage Society production, two nights of Henry James's *The Reprobate* at the Court. Again, this was a box office gamble only a

---

[68] *Tatler*, 15 Oct 1919
[69] Dean, programme for Meggie Albanesi Matinee, Basil Dean Archive
[70] *Daily Telegraph*, 21 Oct 1919
[71] *Observer*, 26 Oct 1919

subscription society would contemplate. No production of James had ever succeeded commercially and *Guy Domville* was a notorious flop. A.B. Walkley's parody shows the ghost of Henry James agonizing over the invitation to attend, implying that *The Reprobate* was an even bigger risk in 1919 than in the 1890s.

> It was monstrous that [the theatre] should be entirely refitted with electric light. And in the crude glare of that powerful illuminant – with every switch or whatever mercilessly turned – didn't they call it? – 'on,' he seemed to see the wretched thing, bare and hideous, with no cheap artifice of 'make-up', no dab of rouge or streak of burnt cork spared the dishonour of exposure. The crack in the golden bowl would be revealed, his awkward age would be brought up against him.....[72]

As Walkley's phantom James realises, a play using stock Edwardian conventions – compromising letters, a Woman with a Past – might seem dated. Walkley's skit also pinpoints a major problem: Jamesian sentence structure needs a reader's eye with all the proliferating clauses in plain view to make sense of it, rather than an audience lulled into inattention and fated to miss the punchlines. The producer was a man passionate about James, Allan Wade. He refused to cut the text, but he had one great virtue – the play made him laugh and he could share the laughter: the cast, he felt, 'entered into the fun of the thing with spirit'.[73]

The Reprobate of the title, 'steeped to the lips in vice.... he had changed his name, he had waxed his moustache...',[74] is a young man who after a harmless fling has been hypnotised by his legal guardians into thinking he must be shut away from the world. He is pursued by Nina, a music-hall singer, and the innocent Blanche Amber, played by Meggie in a saffron dress to suit her name. All the guardians, plus a Northern MP, are pursuing various attachments across a series of intrigues; the actors need fast-moving farce techniques to enliven entrances and exits that are well timed but only just conceal that not much is really happening.

Athene Seyler, who had won the Bancroft Gold Medal seven years before Meggie, played Nina with such dash that her career blossomed. She went on, literally, to write the book on high comedy, stressing the need to involve the whole body and to attend above all to the rhythm of the speech, treating comic dialogue as a game of tennis with each player 'returning the ball good and hard'.[75] The 1880s costumes were sufficiently distanced to make the play a costume piece to be given the gloss of classic high comedy, and the cast treated it as such to impart the speed and brio that it needed – even in over-elaborate exchanges such as

> PAUL ... I shouldn't wonder if I were taking cold!
> BLANCHE What of that? You won't, at least, have vegetated. (*Then as she goes)* I shall!
> PAUL Where are you going?
> BLANCHE To study to be a cabbage!
> PAUL Well, it's simpler!
> BLANCHE Oh, I shall be simple. I should say the penny kind.[76]

---

[72] A.B.Walkley, *Pastiche and Prejudice,* (Heinemann 1921), 60
[73] Quoted by Leon Edell, *The Complete Plays of Henry James* (Rupert Hart-Davis 1949), 402
[74] *The Reprobate ,* Edell, 414
[75] Athene Seyler, *The Craft of Comedy* (NHB1990), 47
[76] James, Edell, 426

To find a solution to the mix of laboured lines and sweet innocence takes the kind of gift Meggie had displayed in Lady Teazle. Alongside the sharper and more worldly wit of Seyler she was, as the *Sunday Times* put it, 'sedately refreshing'.[77]

The ensemble work paid off. *The Reprobate* had a reception kindlier than a James play had achieved since *The American* in 1891 and for perhaps the first time James got credit for theatrical as opposed to purely literary virtues. *The Times* praised its 'bustle and snap'.[78] Even Bernard Shaw quite liked it.

Meanwhile, Meggie's social life was opening out. The dance craze continued: the new conversation-opener was 'do you jazz?' Like many of her generation, she was addicted to movement. In her case, perhaps, it blurred the line between life and performance, and it was in performance that she felt most at ease with herself. New venues sprang up to cater for the young men who had been demobbed only to find themselves out of a job; their money did not stretch to dinner, but the better-off could afford to dance all night. There were the Grafton Galleries, patronised by the Prince of Wales; after 2 a.m. you could go on to Murray's on the river, or risk a police raid and buy a drink at the rather sleazier Rector's in a basement in the Tottenham Court Road, permeated by the smell of its free dead-white face powder.

Meggie's friend Betty Chester, a lively soubrette who worked extensively with the slick pierrot revue company, the Co-Optimists, was cast in *The Knight of the Burning Pestle* with Noel Coward; frustrated by his lack of post-war progress and with several unperformed plays under his belt, Coward took to Meggie at once. He was almost solvent, having sold his first script, and had a brand new tail suit in which he felt 'smart and soigné and very, very smooth'.[79] He took her dancing, sometimes slipping into the Savoy by the back way to avoid the price of a ticket. They evolved a system that allowed them to dine affordably: he ordered, she looked flustered and faint and declared herself unable to swallow a mouthful, and they split the single dish between them with all bread rolls they could snaffle.

Inevitably, there were tensions at home. In the days when living in the West End was affordable on a not-very-lavish actor's salary (Ellen Terry lived in St Martin's Lane, Ivor Novello at Aldwych) the Albanesi home at Lancaster Gate seemed distant and the Albanesis themselves all too present. Carlo was possessive and peppery; he worked a long day, he needed the discipline of routine for his own piano practice and his daughter's returns at the end of an evening performance were disturbing enough; if, as she generally did, she went out until the early hours, suspicion followed as the night the day. For her, the period after midnight that Ivor Novello called 'the actor's playtime' – he founded the 50/50 club specifically to cater for working performers – was necessary to unwind; the hours after a performance were almost invariably a time of bleak self-doubt when she wanted company.

She moved first into a small flat carved out for her in the house; then she left altogether. This was not, though, a reflection of confidence in her economic future. The *Weekly Scotsman* carried an interview where she spoke of the uncertainty of her profession – a theme recurring whenever she talked to the press; she joked that she might join a circus in 'tights and ballet skirts and spangles'.[80] The twenties were about to begin, however; in the theatre Meggie and Noel Coward would define them, although she was only to have a few years in which to do so.

---

[77] *Sunday Times*, 22 Dec 1919
[78] *The Times*, 15 Dec 1919
[79] Noel Coward, *Present Indicative* (Methuen 1986), 80
[80] *Weekly Scotsman*, 20 Dec 1919

'Better be real first'
1920

Post-war drama lacked a clear identity; so did most West End theatres, drifting from musical to serious play to farce in pursuit of cash. The Queen's, however, tried to establish a policy of its own. Alfred Butt, who had controlled eight theatres during the war, and given the Queen's its first long run with *Potash and Perlmutter,* was attempting to consolidate his hold by sharing the management with an actor of stature. In Owen Nares the Queen's had a star who could impress upon it a style grounded in his own stage presence, as Irving and Du Maurier did for the Lyceum and Wyndham's.

Nares was beautiful. His profile was as clear as a cameo, his looks golden-blonde. Throughout his life he was to find himself, alongside Ivor Novello, on lists of 'handsomest stars' or 'most popular actors'. 'He ought to be on the stage,' Tree pronounced on meeting him, 'he's got a Greek head.'[81] But the Greek head was a problem; it was not empty enough for a matinee idol. Self-deprecating and intelligent, Nares was beginning to feel trapped into the sort of career he dreaded. His health was fragile and he had been declared unfit for military service. One of the few available young men with so many actors at the Front, he spent his war drudging away as an object of desire in *Pamela* (young man in love) *Old Heidelberg* (prince in love) and *Romance* (clergyman in love). There are countless photographs of Nares in the same attitude: upstage knee on chaise-longue, downstage foot on floor, forming an elegant diagonal to a swooning lady he clutches with troubled intensity.

It was a critical commonplace that Nares was underrated. Press sideswipes attributed the monotony of his repertoire to 'ladies who only go to see him act in order that they may shut their eyes and put themselves in the heroine's place while Mr. Nares is uttering impassioned things'[82] but the same critics ignored his best qualities, which ran counter to the fashionable acting virtues of his time. His quiet, downbeat Prince Hal opposite Tree's Falstaff in 1914 did not suit the prevailing jingoism, although in a year or so such a reluctant hero might have seemed recognisable and sympathetic to men on leave from the trenches. Nares's Cromwell to Tree's Wolsey was castigated for 'the curiously ultra-modern note in his voice that unfits him for Shakespearean plays',[83] but might have made sense to Granville Barker a few years before or Nigel Playfair a few years later.

In 1919 the Nares-Butt partnership played safe with *The Cinderella Man*, described by Punch as 'syrup by the quart'.[84] At the beginning of 1920 they essayed

---

[81] Owen Nares, *Myself – And Some Others (*Duckworth 1925)
[82] Queen's Theatre Archive, Theatre Museum, unattributed.
[83] *Era,* 7 July 1915
[84] *Punch*, 21 June 1919

a compromise between romance and modernity with Walter Hackett's *Mr. Todd's Experiment.* It was, inevitably, a love story. Arthur John has lapsed into melancholia, wrecking his life and career; his benevolent uncle employs Mr Todd, a psychiatrist, no less, who with sensory stimuli triggers flashbacks to the romantic rejections that have caused it. Arthur John revisits three former loves, before realising his heart belongs to faithful Fancy, a role Hackett wrote for his wife. A review snidely remarked, 'Mr Nares makes love to four different women, seven different times...surely as good as a feast even to the hungry spinster's soul.'[85]

The four women were nineteenth-century clichés: virginal innocent, married vamp, woman with a past and healthy good sport. The *mis-en-scène,* however, offered a spice of modernism by staging Arthur John's thoughts. It sought to create an equivalent of filmic conventions like flashback and the split screen; but rather than using a neutral space to encourage the audience to work out what was happening, it divided the stage into sections, each with a realistic location for the relevant memory. This made for a set so cluttered it allowed no scope for movement, and still managed to confuse some of the audience.

Meggie's role, however, had something that she could seize upon. She played – as the exposition has it – 'Elise Merridew the famous actress who is playing now at the Rubicon Theatre!' Abandoned by Arthur John in the course of a moth-eaten Edwardian plot about jealousy and gipsy rings, Elise survives to make a success of her professional life. She refuses to take him back at the price of renouncing a career 'built on my tears'. The feeble Arthur John cannot face a marriage in which *he* is the failure. If this sequence did not exactly pull the text kicking and screaming into the twenties it at least hinted the pre-war New Woman had not been snuffed out. It brings a welcome moral and emotional complexity into a series of predictable moments.

Meggie and Nares proved a promising partnership. Production photographs of an earlier sequence show Nares in regulation pose, upstage knee on the sofa, etc., while Marie Polini (Mrs Nares) in the substantial role of the married vamp 'registers' emotion (it is not clear which one exactly). All too clearly the policy of multiple settings involves furniture on a reduced scale, so that they seem to be struggling not to fall off a sofa no bigger than a generous armchair. In contrast the photographs of Nares and Meggie seem relaxed and spontaneous; they talk in a self-contained circle of attention of their own making, their eye contact so intent that the watcher is drawn to their faces, not the flimsy and undersized backdrop.

It was a high-status production and the box office was promising. On the first night the great and the good packed the dress circle and the queue for the pit and gallery started at 6 a.m. There was an audible gasp at Nares's entrance. He had opted to subvert his matinee idol status with a bedraggled appearance to suit his hero's self-pity and, worse, a scruffy beard. In the 1920s, such an appendage could draw catcalls in the street. Some fans booed audibly, annoyed that he wasn't offering the mixture as before.

Unfairly, he was still accused by the critics of giving fans 'the time of their sweet sentimental lives'.[86] More column inches were devoted to the beard than the performance. Meggie took most of the acting honours for the fierce integrity she brought to Elise. 'She did hardly more than flash into view and be gone,' remembered W.A.Darlington years later, 'but there was in that fleeting glimpse

[85] Queen's Theatre Archive, Theatre Museum (V&A)
[86] Queen's Theatre Archive, Theatre Museum (V&A)

something that set me groping and peering in the darkness to find her name in the programme.'[87] The play ran for only 67 performances. In the meantime, at last, Meggie had said yes to Basil Dean.

Dean had worked as an actor for the dynamic Annie Horniman who created the noted repertory company at the Manchester Gaiety. He went on to spearhead the Liverpool Company that had grown out of Horniman's success, before tussles with the board of directors led him to quit and work for Tree just before the outbreak of war. Hanging around waiting for demobilisation he received an offer from a sympathetic supporter on the Liverpool board, Alec Rea. A prosperous coal merchant, Rea offered to put up the capital for a new company under Dean's direction, one which would bring to the West End the values and standards of the successful reps: a commitment to new writing; plays chosen for quality rather than for commercial potential; a semi-permanent company to develop and grow from working together; a coherent approach to design.

Dean had been to Berlin to study the work of Max Reinhardt; he was particularly attracted to the way Reinhardt explored the possibilities of electric light rather than treating it as a substitute for gas, but he also absorbed Reinhardt's understanding of theatre as a place where movement and design, acting, dance, music and mime were drawn together. Eclectic in his choice of plays and playwrights, Reinhardt was one of the first directors to attract audiences to his work rather than that of his leading actor. The new company, ReandeaN, called for 'unity of style and purpose, expressed by actors, musicians, artists and technicians, all equally concerned with bringing and author's work to life upon the stage'.[88]

If this sounds uncontroversial in the days of subsidised theatres, it was new in a West End of speculative managements and actors facing an uncertain post-war future. The establishment of a permanent base when Rea signed the lease to the St Martin's added extra energy to the manifesto: at last, a playhouse was to have a declared policy. And this was a new playhouse, only completed in 1916, waiting for an identity.

By the time Meggie joined ReandeaN there had been teething troubles. Dean had settled for a softly-softly opening with undemanding comedies and had four flops in a row. Then, suddenly, it all came together. Dean had a contract for a new play by Galsworthy, whose work had ensured the success of the Manchester Gaiety and who was warmly supportive of the new venture. *The Skin Game* was written at speed in the summer of 1919. Galsworthy interrupted his work on the 'Forsyte' novel *In Chancery,* and some of this irresistible burst of creative energy is apparent in the drive of the play, fuelled by Galsworthy's loathing of war.

The conflict between the self-made Hornblowers grabbing the land of the Hillcrist gentry and the Hillcrists' vicious use of sexual blackmail against them makes an absorbing story. But it also embodies the situation of many who had fought for their country and found both the old landed families and the new capitalist class equally prepared to sacrifice them in a land that was supposed to be fit for heroes. When the play opened on 21 April some of the audience grasped this – one lamented that Galsworthy was ' "out with a hatchet", cutting down beliefs and faiths and leaving the world bare'[89] but many found that the play chimed with their own sense of the post-war world. The applause was tremendous; Galsworthy made

---

[87] *Daily Telegraph*, 13 Dec 1923
[88] Dean, *Seven Ages*, 131
[89] H.V.Marriott, *Life and Letters of John Galsworthy* (Heinemann 1935), 495

a speech in which he remarked that he had been in his box all evening, not 'as an author should be on a first night, wandering among the lions in Trafalgar Square.'[90] Even before the notices, he was probably aware that *The Skin Game* was to be his first commercial success. It eventually ran for 349 performances.

Meggie's performance was a major factor in that success. As Jill Hillcrist she had the most developed role among the younger characters who are the heart and conscience of the play. Jill and Rolf Hornblower have been likened to Romeo and Juliet, but they are a Romeo and Juliet so exasperated by the behaviour of their respective parents, so hurt on their behalf as the conflict grows dirtier, that love is pushed to one side. Jill's language is slangy, fragmented, and full of direct challenges – to her parents, to the Hornblowers, and Rolf. Her honesty is ferocious. 'I only want to be friendly,' says Rolf. 'Better be real first,' replies Jill.[91]

The moral authority Meggie had brought to Elise and Sonia was now allied to an unmistakable modernity; this was one of the first roles to embody post-war youth, the energy, the irreverence, the sense of betrayal and the new way of speaking and moving and behaving; others would follow – notably Noel Coward – but Meggie was the first to give it shape. Critics responded to the way she brought out Jill's charm – 'kittenishly playful',[92] 'adorable',[93] 'the type of young Englishwoman which Mr. Galsworthy can draw better than any other living writer, perfectly painted by Miss Meggie Albanesi.'[94] Her style had greater impact through contrast; the older characters on both sides of the class war are Edwardian in what they say and do; Dean's choice of established West End stars Helen Haye and Edmund Gwenn showed the best of that older, more declamatory style in direct juxtaposition to that of the younger players. Athole Stewart, who played Jill's father, had great sympathy for Meggie's naturalistic approach; they remained friends (she called him 'Dodo' after his character) and he later became a noted exponent of Stanislavsky.

What Dean found in Meggie's performance went beyond contemporaneity; he called it 'an extraordinary quality of stillness'.[95] The *Sunday Express* reviewer concurred. He devoted a good deal of space to analysing the newcomer, a review that seemed designed to cement her reputation as a West End star rather than the darling of the stage societies: 'Miss Meggie Albanesi has been so persistently praised that I had begun to think she must be a thoroughly bad actress. It was a pleasure to find her brimful of talent;' despite the strange criticism that she 'stood on her ankles' he was unreserved in his praise for her quality of 'rapture'.[96]

There are no moments in *The Skin Game* one could describe as happy. The word is clearly used here not in the sense of joy, but of concentration, the state of being 'rapt'. Stillness and rapt concentration are not qualities intrinsic to Jill as a character: she is lively, sporty, headstrong. Rather, the term expresses what Meggie brought to any role. It goes beyond characterisation to the relationship forged between actor and audience; this is not created by the technical aspects of a role: it does not depend on direct address, or even on eliciting a particular response, such as laughter or tears, to an action or a line. Rather, it is a bond made in a silence

---

[90] *Westminster Gazette*, 22 April 1920
[91] Galsworthy, *The Skin Game,* in *Five Plays* (Methuen 1984), 299
[92] *Daily Mail*, 22 April 1920
[93] *Co-Operative News*, 8 May 1920
[94] *Sunday Graphic*, 1 May 1920
[95] Dean, *Seven Ages*, 139
[96] *Sunday Express*, 1 May 1920

which draws spectators into the fact of theatre itself; it transforms the specificities of text and space into something living, created by everyone present, but focussed through a single individual. There was a growing awareness, on both sides of the auditorium, that in Meggie this focus co-existed with the voice of a new generation.

ReandeaN was not out of the woods, but the ingredients of success were in place. The St Martin's was one of the most beautiful and intimate theatres in London. Instead of gilded plaster curlicues it was austerely panelled in warm woods, which gave the impression of a hall in a large house staging a private entertainment. With a capacity of only 550 and a layout that brought all the audience close to the stage, it was a perfect setting for the unstrained naturalism Dean did well (in *The Skin Game* it was like an extension of the world of the play).

The process of forging a company identity was also well advanced. Dean's first appointment had been not an actor but a designer. He had worked with George Harris in Liverpool, where they bonded over a mutual loathing of drooping canvas borders and unconvincing backdrops. Harris gave the productions uncluttered, airy space with artwork that supported the action; he designed a company logo, which stamped ReandeaN publicity and programmes with a clear identity. This was an unusually democratic company in that technical artists were treated as a department in their own right, with a voice in the decision-making process, rather than adjuncts to the director.

Though Dean had, and always would, employ guest performers, the nucleus of the permanent company created by *The Skin Game* was shaping his vision of what could be achieved next. He had three promising players who would remain after the play: Malcolm Keen, an actor with a beautiful voice although Dean felt him badly in need of guidance in intricate roles: Mary Clare, who joined to play Chloe, the vulnerable young woman with a past, widely praised for the warmth she brought to what could have been a dated cliché; Meggie, whose presence would attract others and who was already a trigger for the development of new plays by writers who would link themselves with ReandeaN.

Dean was both the weakness and the strength of the enterprise. He had energy and vision. He was alive to technical innovations that made stages into modern spaces where actors could live and move rather than moth-eaten Victorian backdrops for emotion behind a row of footlights. His broad left sympathies gave him a natural affinity with leading pre-war writers like Galsworthy and Masefield and he made good use of these contacts; they trusted him, gave him first refusal of new scripts and were happy to discuss their work in rehearsal. He had few preconceptions about what made for good drama and was willing to explore theatrical styles from expressionism to symbolism, although he was less sure-footed when he moved away from the naturalistic social-problem plays that had made his name.

On the other hand he was notoriously difficult; some felt, perhaps rightly, that he was a shy man; but his management style meant that he was widely known as 'Bastard Basil'; rumours abounded of his cruelty to actors, of performers fainting after a Dean tongue-lashing, or driven to suicide. He once reduced Olivier to tears. Noel Coward listed 'all his artillery – gentle sarcasm, withering contempt, sharp irascibility and occasionally full-throated roaring'.[97] There are so many stories that it seems as if being bullied by Dean could be considered as much rite of passage for actors as carrying a spear. The playwright Moss Hart related an incident when he

[97] Noel Coward, *Present Indicative* (Methuen 1986), 184

was a young actor waiting in the stalls at a Dean rehearsal hoping for an interview. One older actor was visibly struggling: Dean concentrated on the others, saving the following interchange for the end of the day:

> 'Would you mind doing that again?' he said, addressing the character man directly for the first time.
> 'Do what again, Mr Dean?'
> 'Why, that splendid bit of acting you were perpetrating just now,' replied Mr Dean with a sweetness that was almost purring. The character man moved his tongue over his lips. 'I'm pleased you thought so, Mr. Dean,' he said with a hollow little laugh. 'I'm rather fond of that bit myself. I wondered if you would notice it.'
> 'Notice it?' said Mr Dean. 'Indeed, indeed! I have been riveted. He smiled dangerously at the character man. 'In my many years in the theatre, ladies and gentlemen,' he said, 'I have witnessed and been subjected to many kinds of acting, and of course, styles of acting change. I do not cherish tradition and I welcome innovation, but I have been greatly puzzled this last few minutes... I've never seen anything quite like our colleague's performance before, and since I think it unlikely that we shall ever see anything like it again, I suggest that you all come to the front with me and watch it…'[98]

It seems typical of Dean that he simmered over Hart's account for some years, using the last volume of his autobiography to justify himself; even more typical that what he thought needed justification was his failure to employ Hart (who claimed to have abandoned acting after identifying with the character man). His sadistic-schoolmaster technique, though, he seemed to consider perfectly legitimate.

The anecdote suggests that his habit was to wait to see what a performer had to offer and to seize upon what worked. If this meant that sometimes he didn't know what he wanted and was peevish until he got it, it could also, given his often intelligent casting against type, make an actor reach inside himself and produce something interesting and fresh. Coward, who stood up to Dean while still a child and was never one to be intimidated, broke down while playing in *The Constant Nymph* but valued Dean's refusal to allow him any personal mannerisms and was widely praised in the role. Gielgud wrote of the directing talent of the twenties that 'there are only four or five of whom any of us would say, "I should like to be produced by him" …Komisarjevsky, Guthrie and Dean.'[99]

If only the talented dared work with Dean, that was one way of maintaining standards. He was, too, able to transmit something of the excitement of a shared and worthwhile enterprise to the ReandeaN regulars; through the next few years they were to develop a strong identity and build an audience, and this made for confidence in a shaky economic climate.

In Meggie he had a performer with whom he felt instinctively in tune. He was clear about where the responsibility for her work lay. 'With each successive production, sympathy and understanding grew between us, until at last people behind the scenes used jokingly to talk about Trilby and Svengali. This was absurd.

---

[98] Moss Hart, *Act One* (Secker and Warburg 1960), 110

[99] Jonathan Croall, *Gielgud: A Theatrical Life* (Methuen 2000), 192 (Gielgud was only willing to name three, but as Croall suggests, he may well have considered himself the fourth.)

Meggie was always herself, selecting carefully what little help I could give her, rejecting the unsuitable. Throughout her work with us I never once heard her give a false inflection.'[100]

The relationship undoubtedly had its own effect on the company's rehearsal atmosphere and style. If a company is close-knit, a clear image of what is going right energises the whole group. Dean's ruthless clearing of dead wood might make space for success to flourish if given a more positive counterbalance. Meggie, like others who were to be absorbed into the company, had excellent social skills. The warmth they generated prevented Dean's clutter-clearing from becoming excessively painful. Dean was the director of ReandeaN, but the regular players like Meggie, the technical team under George Harris and the kind Alec Rea were as responsible for the company style.

If the next productions did not match the success of *The Skin Game,* the long run meant that there was an ongoing reminder to London of what ReandeaN could achieve. And towards the end of the run the company had an additional fillip to morale: a film of the production. *The Skin Game* was hardly an obvious choice in the silent movie era. But the backer, who ran a Staffordshire factory, responded to this story of land versus kilns and chimneys and set up the Anglo-Hollandia Company specially to make it with the Granger-Binger Film Company, using the original cast.

The rate at which it evolved looks, in contrast to the development hells of today, like a piece of speeded up film itself. B.E.Doxatt-Pratt started developing the scenario in late August; by December he was holding a midnight wrap party for the cast, who journeyed up to the Potteries for location work; they shot two hundred scenes, against the kilns of the Armitage factory at Tunstall and out in the countryside where Meggie gave Jill a little sporting colour by riding side-saddle. They failed to set the British film industry on fire, although there was some interest in the North. Liverpool expressed enthusiasm for a project by a director of their own Repertory Theatre and showed the film at the Futurist. It was never more than an attempt to provide the provinces with a glimpse of one of the most popular plays in London, but it gave the cast a pleasant interlude.

Meggie considered that she was going stale in the role of Jill, and was keen to take up an opportunity to work with a different management for a short break. Dean was sympathetic to the idea of a transfer and gave interviews in which he proclaimed ReandeaN's progressive attitude in taking care of its own by allowing such changes. She went to the Comedy to play the role of a half-Italian princess in *The Charm School.*

Alice Duer Miller's novel had appeared in 1919. Its breathless description of the hero made its dramatisation inevitable, and the casting equally so: 'The young man was of the most extraordinary beauty – not only of face, but of figure, for he was as lithe and active as a cat, but his conspicuous feature was his eyes – eyes of the clearest sky blue…a mouth of sensitive curves…and a chin that contradicted these curves by its firm aggression.'[101] Even for those who had missed their brief moment at the Queen's, the partnership of Meggie and Owen Nares sounded attractive.

The dramatisation added a wise-cracking secretary to bring a little acidity to the script but it still had enormous potential to be embarrassingly saccharine. Nares

---

[100] Dean, *Seven Ages*, 222
[101] Alice Duer Miller, *The Charm School* (Hodder and Stoughton 1919), 7

played a young car salesman who inherits a school; he decides to apply the marketing principle of giving the public what it wants – and parents 'want their daughters turned into charming women – marriageable women'. His reforms include getting rid of uniforms and pigtails (in the era of the shingle Meggie, who could sit on her hair in the tradition of Edwardian beauties, was the only one not to need a wig) bringing in pretty dresses, and gently discouraging his pupils from aspirations towards college. Meanwhile, Elise, the head girl, discreetly hunts him. The description of Elise is enough to set off warning bells. 'They were wonderful eyes – soft, dark and large as pansies, set in a lovely little face turned up to him with the look of a worshipper to a saint.'[102] For Nares, there was a welcome edge of self-mockery in a hero who would prefer to look more like a sound businessman than a Greek god; but Meggie's role had the sentimentality of those lines running through it like a stick of Blackpool rock.

She ignored it. She chose to assume that however feeble the language the love was genuine. The critics could find nothing to praise in the text and the reviews were a series of variations on 'sugary', 'sickly', 'nauseous', but they responded to the vitality of the stage presence that interpreted it. W.G Royde-Smith recalled that 'she made the poor thing beautiful by playing it stark and hard, without curls or dimples (these indeed she could never assume with any hope of success)…she made it almost a tragedy, so great was the emotional power she put into it.'[103]

There was, as yet, no common vocabulary in which a critic could dissect the process of characterisation, but there is an illuminating distinction here. Meggie's performance did not depend on external aspects of the character ('curls or dimples' sound appalling, but there are other attributes of physical charm that could be substituted); rather it focussed on what Elise desired, what Stanislavsky called the super-objective. The play never approaches 'tragedy' in that it has a happy ending and is too fluffy for us to expect anything else, but what is possible, and what Meggie was clearly able to bring to it, was risk. The character does have things to lose: not only her chosen lover, but, as she takes all the initiatives, her own dignity if her courtship fails.

A photograph of the production shows Nares seated at his desk on an important-looking chair, studiously ignoring her. She is curled on a bench, wearing an elegant dress that he has prescribed in the place of the school uniform, her head a little to one side so that he is forced into eye contact. It is an opportunity to flirt, or to look cute, and she has chosen to reject it. Rather, she looks at him with gravity, as if the issue they are speaking of is something vital. Nigel Playfair had recently invited her to play Rosalind at the Lyric. She refused, saying that she felt that she was not yet ready, and the role went to the more experienced Athene Seyler. Playfair did not press her, considering that her decision showed maturity.

There would have been other opportunities; the Lyric's reputation for imaginative classical productions shone through the decade and added lustre to the reputations of Gielgud and Edith Evans. But the photograph suggests *As You Like It* was still on her mind; there is a definite flavour of Rosalind and Orlando in this frozen moment; it is the point in the play when Elise tells the young headmaster she loves him. This was Meggie's first real leading role in a romantic comedy and her approach looks as if she was trying a kind of rough draft of the role she had rejected. Her body language suggests she is serenely claiming her territory, relaxed on her

---

[102] Miller, *The Charm School.* 56
[103] *Weekly Westminster Gazette,* 15 Dec 1923

1. With Owen Nares in *The Charm School,* December 1920

bench as if it were not designed to stress her role as subordinate schoolgirl; she is clearly the one who understands the situation, looking directly into Nares's eyes with a shattering honesty.

It was a moment to which the audience warmed; they praised her 'beautifully natural handling of her scenes of sentiment'[104]; 'an exquisite piece of work',[105] wrote

[104] *Illustrated London News*, 8 Jan 1921
[105] *Daily Telegraph*, 24 Dec 1920

the *Telegraph*; and, in a word that accorded oddly with the soppiness of the text, they praised her restraint. For the first time, she was receiving credit for the intelligence she brought to her work; her earlier roles had varied in importance and had offered her excellent opportunities which she had visibly taken. But through the wafer-thin writing of *The Charm School* it was possible to see the traps in wait for a less thoughtful performer. Her 'naturalness' was not the function of a well-planned subtext but something that depended on careful judgement, a belief in the character's situation and a refusal to read sentimental lines sentimentally. 'Meggie Albanesi took the absurd creature and turned her into a human being who mattered intensely not less to us than to herself – and that was a piece of sheer acting-magic,'[106] wrote W.A. Darlington much later.

None of this would have been possible without the support of Nares. It would have been easy to emphasise the role of the hero as a kindly mentor, to patronise Elise until she looked as absurd as the text makes her. Instead, he took what he must have realised was a back seat. As the *Telegraph* put it: '[Elise] is lucky, no doubt – but not so lucky as he is; for the head girl is played by Miss Meggie Albanesi, and very beautifully too. If Mr. Nares did think of setting up a school for teaching girls charm in real life the first thing he ought to do should be to secure Miss Albanesi – not as head girl but as instructress.'[107] Nares allowed 'instructress' its full weight, and stressed the immature and boyish aspects of the young headmaster, letting Meggie-as-Elise do the teaching about love as if they were in the Forest of Arden; there was no foot-planted-on-the-chaise-longue nonsense. The tentativeness, the lack of dominance, made him the genuinely modern lover that he had wanted to be in *Mr Todd's Experiment*.

The play opened just before Christmas Eve, offering itself as an unpretentious holiday treat. But the sense of Arden was not wasted on the critics. J.T. Grein remarked 'It is all as light as a feather and as fantastic as if the world were an Eden instead of a vale of tears. But it lays hold of you.'[108] In the silly play Meggie and Nares had both found new aspects of their talent, aspects they would bring to better roles in the coming year.

---

[106] *Daily Telegraph*, 13 Dec 1923
[107] *Daily Telegraph*, 24 Dec 1920
[108] *Illustrated London News*, 22 Jan 1921

‘The modern young girl’
1921

ReandeaN’s fortunes were still fluctuating. Dean had felt confident enough to make a policy statement: the company would not only specialise in new drama, but the plays would be specifically British;[109] he backed this up by mounting a second production during the run of *The Skin Game* – *The Blue Lagoon,* a spectacular show which included a boat being tossed on realistic stormy seas and Faith Celli in a very small dress. It ran to full houses at the Prince of Wales.

However, *The Skin Game’s* replacement, *The Wonderful Visit*, which opened in February 1921, was a failure. It was the first ReandeaN flop that was not a consequence of timidity; adapted by St John Ervine from a novel by H.G.Wells, it had a popular writer and high-quality visual effects; but one of the principals had an ageing memory and lost her place. The incoherence of the first night proved box office poison and Dean searched for a new script. This time, however, he avoided the timidity of the previous year. He chose a new British play he considered ‘would have stood no chance of acceptance by a commercial management’,[110] Clemence Dane’s *A Bill of Divorcement.*

Dane was the kind of writer for whom ReandeaN had come into existence. Born in 1888, she belonged to the new post-war playwrights rather than the Shaw-Galsworthy-Barrie era. In her seventies, still vital and still working, she compared her generation with Osborne’s – for both, she felt, social and political conditions had necessitated ‘inevitably, dramas of revolt’.[111] Her grasp of theatre, like Reinhardt’s disciple Dean, was holistic and practical. She had trained at the Slade, and continued to sculpt and paint in oils (her best-known surviving work is a bust of Noel Coward in the National Portrait Gallery). She had worked as an actress, under the name Diana Cortis, in fluffy dramas with titles like *Oh, I Say!* She was already a published novelist and held strong feminist opinions (in 1926 she brought out a book called *The Woman’s Sid*e urging women to enter all spheres of public life). Coward based the character of Madame Arcati in *Blithe Spirit* on Dane – earnest, energetic and given to *doubles-entendres* which he, perhaps mistakenly, assumed to be unintentional.

It is worth bearing in mind that Madame Arcati gets her own way, and Dane’s political convictions and personality were strong enough to allow her to stand up to Dean when necessary, even though *A Bill of Divorcement* was her first completed play. She had been working on *Will Shakespeare*, a long verse drama that ReandeaN also produced in November 1921, but felt sufficiently pressured from within by the ideas in *Bill of Divorcement* to abandon Shakespeare for six weeks in

---

[109] *The Times*, 14 Dec 1920
[110] Dean, *Seven Ages*, 143
[111] Clemence Dane, Presidential Address to the English Association July 1961, 9

the summer of 1920. The speed of composition, as Dane pointed out, showed that the play had been fermenting in her mind for a long time; it owed a great deal to her own novel *Legend*.

The post-war years saw many transformations in the lives of women and some of the most far-reaching involved changes in the laws of divorce. The Asquith government had appointed a Royal Commission on Divorce and Matrimonial Causes in 1909. After eleven years it produced four volumes of evidence, still regarded as essential reading on the subject; its general tenor met considerable controversy although the suggested reforms were hardly sweeping. This year it would be possible to obtain a divorce after five years on the grounds of incurable insanity, or after three for drunkenness; by 1923 it would no longer be necessary for wives to prove cruelty as well as adultery (although cruelty alone would get both parties no more than a legal separation).

Dane, watching the passage of Lord Gorell's Bill through Parliament, saw herself as writing 'propaganda…against those who tried to "crab" [it]'.[112] She set the play in the future, with the law already established, so the dilemmas depicted were moral rather than legal. A couple are about to get married in the teeth of opposition from both church and family. Their situation is not of their own making; the woman's former husband has been shell-shocked in the war and has a genetic propensity for insanity; she has divorced him, assuming that his condition is irrevocable, to find that he has recovered, at least temporarily, and wants her back. Only the self-sacrifice of the daughter allows the new marriage to go forward. Knowing she will inherit her father's illness, she gives up her own engagement and promises to devote her life to caring for him.

It was a piece very much of its time; divorce was to feature in two other plays that year: *The Fulfilling of the Law* and *A Social Convenience*. The topicality ensured the speed at which Dean offered a contract and the play went into rehearsal in February 1921. The casting of Sydney, the daughter, was inevitable. One of the elements in Dane's mind during the process of composition had been Meggie herself. 'Long ago, when the first hazy notion came,'[113] Dane said, 'she and no other' embodied her image of Sydney.

The Charm School was still running. Lilian Braithwaite, Dean's choice for Sydney's mother, was appearing at Wyndham's, and C. Aubrey Smith, contracted to play the mother's strong-minded fiancé, Gray, was rehearsing a new play at the St James's. Rehearsals for *Bill* were an organisational nightmare. They barely began when Meggie contracted the flu doing the rounds of the West End (the comic sailor in *Blue Lagoon* had collapsed on stage) and for two days ran a high fever, which left her exhausted. Rehearsals shifted to her flat, the cast manoeuvring themselves around her bed. Effie inevitably arrived to supervise the care of her daughter and there was a nurse constantly in attendance; the press crowded in and pictures of a wan white-clad Meggie, nurse hovering, appeared in a number of papers along with their good wishes. Though this free publicity helped, the company could not afford to postpone the production. Dean did move the first night from the Saturday to Monday, 14 March, but this still left her extremely weak; she was to play for some days with both doctor and nurse in attendance.

This was partly the natural determination any actor has to make her own first night at all costs; Meggie had it to a marked degree. She also had a remarkably high

[112] *Star*, 15 March 1921
[113] *Star*, 15 March 1921

level of insecurity: she was fully aware how easy it could be for a performer to miss an opportunity, to be replaced by one of thousands waiting for a chance, to slip into obscurity, and she was never really satisfied with her own work, often frustrated by what she considered failure.

But she also had a special relationship with the role, and the cast had one with the play. From the outset, despite squabbles between Dean and Dane, despite Meggie's illness, there seemed to exist a conviction that the play was destined for success. Dean describes 'a family atmosphere' [114] engendered perhaps by a mixture of shared vicissitudes and confidence in the text; they knew that it would cause controversy – *Plain English* announced it would 'destroy Christian marriage'[115] – but this could only be an advantage when it also offered every performer scenes guaranteed to hold an audience.

When it came, though, the success was greater than they could have hoped. The applause was terrific; there were countless curtain calls, for the writer and director as well as for the cast, there was a speech by Clemence Dane; and, finally, chants of 'We want Meggie.' The notices proclaimed, 'this is a play that everybody will be going to see:'[116] the papers ran articles and interviews with everyone in the cast – the *Evening News* even printed one with 'Bill', the Airedale puppy who appeared in Act I; Dane was proclaimed as a phenomenon, a 'Woman Dramatist' – or for the *Evening News,* a 'new girl playwright'. It was, however, Meggie's performance that established the performance as a major theatrical event.

What had drawn Dane to her was not the power she displayed in *The Rising Sun* or *Reparation*, but the surefootedness of her comic timing and her ability to ironize her ridiculous flapper persona in *St. George and the Dragons.* Throughout *Bill of Divorcement* Sydney has space to develop her political and personal attitudes to events; but the news of Hilary's recovery, which shatters both the harmony her mother has achieved with Gray and Sydney's own bright faith in her future, comes early in the action.

There is only a brief opportunity for the audience to see Sydney as a confident and modern seventeen-year-old. Without this, the magnitude of her sacrifice cannot come across. Dane provides a comic opening that means the performer must hit the ground running. Sydney rushes on, opens her Christmas presents and smirks that she has bought her censorious Aunt Hester a cigarette-case so she can trade it back for the prayer-book she has predictably given Sydney. She bustles about organising her mother and Gray, playing with her new puppy, teasing her fiancé Kit and managing her self-appointed role as 'bridesmaid and best man and family lawyer and Juliet's Nurse all rolled into one'.[117] Her comedy returns at the end in more acerbic vein; having decided she can never marry, she stages a row with the vacuous Kit so that he will leave her.

The role demands the style Coward had begun to develop in his first success, *I'll Leave It To You*, which had a short run but excellent reviews in 1920 – self-consciously witty, hard almost to callousness, bubbling with energy rather than languidly epigrammatic in the manner of pre-war comedy. But it also reveals the emotional strain that goes into preserving this kind of front. As a character in Coward's later *Shadow Play* puts it, 'Small talk – a lot of small talk with quite

---

[114] *Seven Ages*, 143
[115] *Plain English,* 17 March 1921
[116] *Bystander*, 27 April 1921
[117] Clemence Dane, *A Bill of Divorcement* (Samuel French Ltd 1948), 18–19

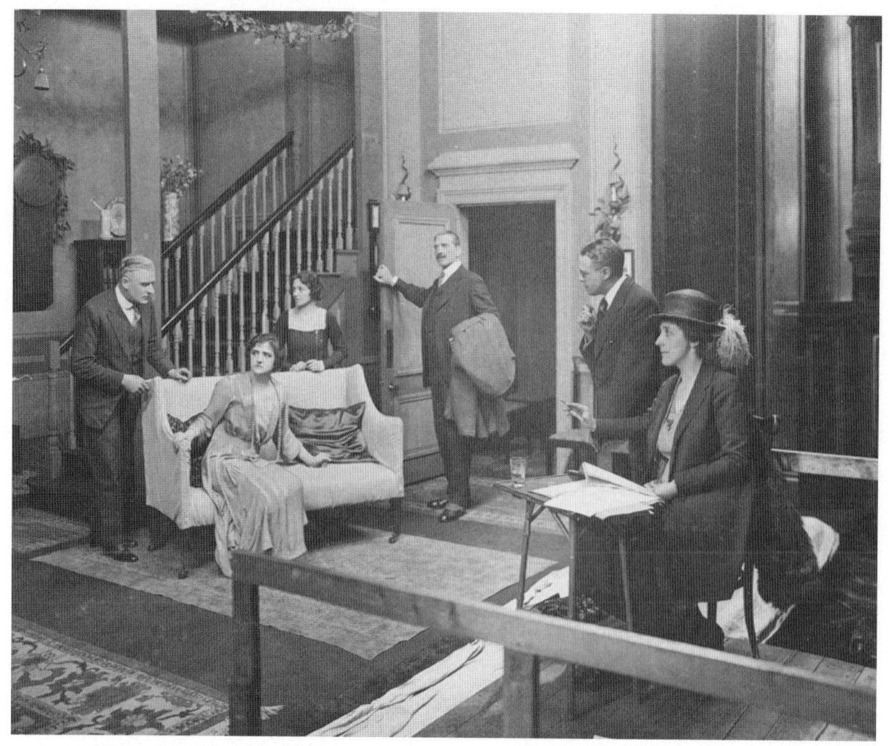

2. Rehearsal for *A Bill of Divorcement,* March 1921. L to R: Malcolm Keen, Lilian Braithwaite, Meggie Albanesi, C. Aubrey Smith, Basil Dean. Clemence Dane

different thoughts going on behind it.'[118] The critics responded to the wit and emotion of Meggie's Sydney, Desmond MacCarthy describing her 'prompt, careless movements, her offhand, clear level tones, her hard little compressed manner, suddenly melting (it is a matter of eyes and a movement of the hands) into that of the affectionate excitable child.'[119]

Coward's next play *The Young Idea* poked gentle fun at *Bill:* his youthful protagonists pretend to have a mad father who 'eats the buttons off padded chairs'. *The Young Idea* established him as the voice of his generation; but it was Meggie and Dane who blazed the trail by tying this comic style to the vulnerability of post-war youth.

Sydney refers to herself as 'twentieth century' and to her mother and Gray as 'nineteenth century'. Overtly, this describes their attitudes to marriage and divorce; but it also indicates performance styles. The major scene between Gray and Margaret, where Margaret struggles with her conscience, tries to renounce him and eventually yields to Sydney's assertions that the care of Hilary 'is my job, not yours', requires a single emotion from the performers. If there is any variety of tone it springs not from any attempt to make light of their suffering but from Gray's increasing anger in pressing his case and Margaret's increasing anguish resisting him; it is the kind of sustained torment that Edwardian society drama did well.

---

[118] Noel Coward, *Shadow Play, Tonight at 8.30,* Play Parade IV (Heinemann 1954)
[119] *New Statesman*, 9 April 1921

In the production stills Lilian Braithwaite adopts a fixed expression throughout, her eyes staring appalled into a terrible future; when her posture is not ramrod straight, she is leaning on the furniture – sometimes as if near collapse, sometimes seeming to push against it as if to dramatise her resistance to the situation. C. Aubrey Smith is invariably bolt upright, both feet braced solidly apart to stress the military bearing his shell-shocked rival has never managed to achieve.

Smith and Braithwaite are working with the grain of the text; as their lines express the thoughts of the characters without ambiguity, so their body language supports it. Although they are meant to be relatively young – Margaret sees herself as a child rushed into a wartime romance and is still in her early thirties – they look older. In Braithwaite's case this is not a matter of clothing or make-up – she is fashionably dressed, her face unlined – but of bearing. For her there is no middle ground between rigidity and near-collapse. It is entirely appropriate to the kind of Edwardian drama which allowed its heroines to choose only between respectable marriage and moral obloquy – the kind of play that has shaped Margaret's imagination and at which Braithwaite herself excelled. (Four years later Coward cast her as the irresponsible mother in *The Vortex* for sheer surprise value.)

This is all designed to contrast with the modernist comedy of Sydney in the early scenes. But the play also demands a development of the naturalism Meggie achieved in *The Rising Sun.* Sydney is the only character revealed primarily through subtext. While she is articulate about her opinions on everything from divorce to eugenics, there are always pressures on her to control, or conceal, or disguise her feelings. When she overhears the scene between Gray and Margaret she has no lines, beyond an exclamation under her breath; she stands on the stairs and listens, and it is for the performer alone to establish how she feels, how she reaches the decision to let her mother go and remain with her father.

Photographs of this moment show marked contrast between Braithwaite and Smith, whose bodies echo the intense pitch of their lines, and Meggie as Sydney, watching in the shadows on the stair. There is no tension in her because she is concentrating on what she sees; she makes no gesture but simply holds Margaret's coat. Dane records that Meggie took a single step down when Margaret expressed complete inability to make up her own mind; she took one more when Gray told Margaret that he would leave her, and let the cloak slip onto the banister.

These are motivated gestures, nothing solely for effect; but the moment created in the audience a tension abruptly snapped by Sydney voicing the decision that they had watched her reach in silence. For the rest of the scene Sydney is galvanising her mother into leaving, trying to develop a bond between herself and her father, and putting up with the censorious Hester – all the while absorbing what the consequences of her decision will mean for her.

And then, the action over, the future was made real in Meggie's body: for a moment, she was left alone onstage listening to Gray's car leaving, while Sydney considers what will come. This was, as Meggie told her mother, a key moment for her, when the gap between her and the role did not seem to exist.[120] The lighting, shifting from sunset to darkness over George Harris's beautiful winter backdrop, supported her performance. She did not need to 'register' an emotion or offer any overt recognition of the situation, but as *The Times* noted, to 'let the *lacrimae rerum* do the rest,'[121] and allow the audience to become conscious of sharing her feelings.

---

[120] *Meggie Albanesi*, 87
[121] *The Times*, 15 March 1921

3. With Ian Hunter in *A Bill of Divorcement,* March 1921

In the last lines of the play, overtly optimistic, her voice briefly broke, the smallest possible signal of what was going on within, but one nobody missed. Desmond MacCarthy, like many others, was especially struck by her delivery of 'Father, don't believe her! I'm not hard, I'm not hard,'[122] remarking 'that wail, that temporary collapse of Sydney's courage, is very moving.'[123] *

For the collapse is temporary, and must be seen to be so; the audience could not bear to believe otherwise. What made Dane's play different from the other fashionable divorce plays of the period was the setting in the future and the context this created. Hilary may have inherited his illness but the shellshock that precipitates it made him a recognisable figure to the post-war generation. In effect, he is a young man, still in his mind living in the 1920s with all the horror of the war uppermost in his thoughts. Malcolm Keen's youthful good looks and thick white hair fitted his carefully studied and widely praised portrayal of symptoms that were all too easy, in 1921, to observe first-hand. Sydney is just as recognisably a young woman of the 1920s, too young to be involved in the War but shaped by her time – atheistic, slangy, independent, presenting an image of tough cynicism, rejecting the values of a generation seen as responsible for the slaughter.

The rapport between Keen and Meggie, the nucleus of the permanent company, was widely praised as evidence of the bond between 'two souls adrift',[124] though the dislocated timeframe of *Bill* makes them father and daughter, with different responsibilities, they stressed their status as counterparts, near-contemporaries (they had been cast as such in *The Skin Game*). Like Escher's picture of two hands drawing each other, the relationship between Sydney and Hilary is an impossible object, which nevertheless made sense to the younger generation. Sydney is both victim and shaper of her times – a cartoon showed Meggie as puppeteer controlling the characters as marionettes [125] – a figure as emblematic of her time as Osborne's Jimmy Porter of his, and with the same career-changing potential for the actor who created the role.

It was this mixture of contemporaneity and dramatic power that underlay Meggie's personal reception. There were other actors to whom the young audiences of the 1920s responded in a way that has come to be associated with rock stars. One was Noel Coward, already finding his wittier remarks were greeted with 'Another Noelism', though he had to wait until *The Vortex* in 1924 to become more than a minority cult. Another was the American actress Tallulah Bankhead, with a husky deep-south accent steeped in sex and a way of turning innocent lines into a kind of erotic code addressed directly to her fans, many of them working-class 'gallery girls' who in turn picked up their cue to call out and cheer.

With both of them, however, the audience rapport had a different relationship to naturalism. Coward vigorously marketed himself as actor, writer, singer, composer and revue artist; while he might sink himself in a role as he did for Dean in *The Constant Nymph* it was hard to be unaware of his endless self-reinvention. Bankhead

---

[122] Dane, *A Bill of Divorcement,*, 92
[123] *New Statesman*, 9 April 1921
[124] *The Lady*, 24 March 1921
[125] *Illustrated Sporting and Dramatic,* 9 April 1921

* Dean also recalls this particular moment as unforgettable (*Seven Ages*, 143) but he makes an interesting Freudian slip, misquoting the line as 'Oh, Mummy, I'm not hard.'

Sydney's mother, of course, has already left at this point. Does this reflect the strained relationship that evolved during those rehearsals while Meggie was confined to bed, a time when Effie felt she should not have been expected to continue working?

could play a naturalistically written role with skill and truth, if she felt like it, but she often preferred to turn a cartwheel, add a topical allusion, or blow a kiss to the gallery girls instead. With Meggie, the roles she played entered more decisively into the equation: they were something she offered the public as a gift because they spoke to their mutual situation. Coward's fans wanted to imitate him. Bankhead's wanted to make love to her. But Meggie's seemed to feel that they already *were* her.

In 1931 Dane published a novel about a dynasty of actors, *Broome Stages.* Throughout its scholarly and entertaining narrative woven around different theatrical styles there runs a consistent conviction about the most basic aspect of performance. The founding father of the Broomes learns a magic spell which he hands down to his descendants. Dane never, of course, reveals it, but tantalises the reader with a snippet – enough to express her conviction about the nature of theatre:

> 'Beckon, Dickon!' he would quote, and protest that the art of acting was but the art of beckoning. And indeed, when the house rose at him as it sometimes did, bodily, with a frightening forward surge, it was as if the whole concourse of tired men and women desired to bathe in the transfiguring theatre light.[126]

'Beckoning' expresses the relationship Dane perceived between Meggie and her audience. It did not involve direct address; rather, it meant donning a character like a ceremonial garment and not only experiencing the emotions of the part but conducting the audience into them too, like Virgil in the underworld, so that they were able not only to feel but to evaluate what they felt.

Post-war youth suddenly had a self-image in Sydney that went beyond frivolity or resentment at the lack of good brave causes left. J.T.Grein suggested that 'the most promising actress of the younger generation' had offered a 'study of the modern young girl with a heart and a will' with an explicitly cathartic function. 'The character of the girl is so splendid, so great, that we came away in elevation instead of sorrow. We feel that the war has bred other stuff than things evil, that in widening the horizon of youth and womanhood it has in some way resuscitated altruism.'[127] 'Gallery Girl' in *The Star* concurred, describing the character Meggie had created as the 'finest type of girl' modern life could produce.[128]

It is a measure of her impact that critics were already attempting to define the nature of her acting style. *The Bookman* usefully contrasted it with Athene Seyler's. Seyler it considered a 'creative' actress, Meggie an 'interpretative' one. 'She seems to have no existence outside the part she is assuming…it overmasters her.'[129] 'Creative' here seems to mean 'inventiveness'. Seyler produced brilliant comic effects through the precision of her body language, a process she described as one of refining something originally spontaneous. 'I am sure,' she later wrote, 'one has to rely first on the subconscious or inspirational method of reading a part by sinking oneself in the character, and then check the results consciously from outside oneself and keep what seems good and discard what seems overdone or misses fire. It's a kind of dual control of one's performance.'[130] For Olivier, as for many others of his generation, the externals of a character came earlier than this and offered the bedrock

---

[126] Clemence Dane, *Broome Stages* (Heinemann 1931), 15
[127] *Illustrated London News,* 2 April 1921
[128] *The Star,* 21 March 1921
[129] *The Bookman*, June 1921
[130] Seyler, *The Craft of Comedy,* 52

of a performance. 'External characteristics to me are a shelter – a refuge from having nothing to feel, from finding yourself standing on the stage with just lines to say.'[131]

Meggie cared little for externals; her clothes tended to come from a single designer and were not very different from her offstage wear; her makeup was restrained, with no attempt to make herself a different face. She did not want shelter on the stage, rather to strip away anything between her and the role, a process of self-emptying the mystics call *kenosis*, leaving her free to beckon her audience into the play. If Olivier feared having nothing to express, Meggie feared being unable to express what she knew she had no choice *but* to express.

This almost religious quality had been celebrated in actors before, most recently in Duse. It had not been previously linked to post-war theatre's approach to youth, family and the times. It was a potent activity for a young performer, and Meggie found that the role continued to exhaust her. The tears, she told a reporter, were real each time. She found that the words carried their own emotional memory, not associated with her own life, but with the feelings she had when she first spoke them; she wasn't sure whether this was a function of inexperience, but 'at present', she could not work off technique alone; she needed to be 'one of those actresses who suffer each time'.[132] She remained alone in her dressing room for some time before a performance and stationed her dresser Patty outside for twenty minutes or so afterwards, before going out to dance herself back into spirits for the rest of the night.

A Bill of Divorcement ran for 401 performances. Audiences continued to pack the theatre. The King and Queen came. Clergymen preached sermons on it. There was even a bootleg production of the play on tour by a bankrupt manager called Albert Leigh, and Dean had to take out a restraining order. He also celebrated ReandeaN's success in a special ReandeaN Pictorial containing a retrospective manifesto. 'Its founders declared…that their chief objects were the production of the best plays by British Authors and the encouragement of unity and coherence in the acting…the following list of plays already produced by ReandeaN Companies shows, we contend, a certain fulfilment of promises made.'[133] All this time, Meggie never willingly took a break from the role; her relationship with it was too strong to give it up to an understudy.

There were a few diversions, however. She retained strong links with Kenneth Barnes and the Academy. He wrote a Sunday night play for her, about a psychiatrist and his patient, but the flu intervened and Flora Robson got her first real chance in the role. In May, she joined in the celebrations as the now-Royal Academy finally got its new theatre in Gower Street, opened by the Prince of Wales. The best-known alumni, including Ion Swinley and Athene Seyler, gave a gala performance on 27 May – the first act of Pinero's *Trelawney of the 'Wells'*, in which Meggie played Rose Trelawney.

This light comedy about struggling actors in the 1860s made an agreeably frothy evening; but it was also a manifesto about acting style. Pinero, writing in 1898, was looking affectionately back at the old mid-Victorian companies with their Walking Gentlemen and impossible Fred Terry heroes, and celebrating the rise of a new British realism and restraint. He was thinking in terms of Robertson, rather than Ibsen or even Du Maurier, but the faith his struggling playwright Tom Wrench

---

[131] Laurence Olivier, *On Acting* (Simon and Schuster 1986),153
[132] *Weekly Dispatch,* 5 June 1921
[133] *ReandeaN Pictorial*, Vol. 1 no 2

proclaims in a 'different order from the old order which is departing',[134] the simpler, less bombastic approach painfully pioneered by Rose, looks forward to the naturalism of the post-war generation.

If Trelawney did prompt reflections about the nature of realism and performance, there was a new ReandeaN experiment in which to explore them. During some complex financial wranglings between Viola Tree and her landlord C.B.Cochran, Dean managed to lease the Aldwych Theatre, where he hoped to house Flecker's *Hassan.* The *Hassan* project had taken years of patient negotiation and was not yet ready; as a holding strategy he invited Owen Nares to join the company for *Love Among the Paint Pots.*

This 'light entertainment for hot weather,' as 'Our Captious Critic'[135] called it, starred Nares as a man emerging from prison (falsely accused, of course) to work as a decorator and find true love. It was not designed to stretch his talent. 'His hair is really beautiful,' sighed *Pan* magazine.[136] Dean did have a genuine respect for Nares and included him in a more challenging play he was presenting for a limited series of Aldwych matinees, Galsworthy's *The First and the Last.* Nares found himself once again partnering Meggie.

The play is an extraordinary mix: the language and setting are naturalistic, but it constantly seems to be pushing towards expressionism. Larry Darrant (Nares), a wastrel and a drinker, takes up with a Polish refugee, Wanda (Meggie) and in a scuffle kills her brutal husband/pimp. He goes for help to his brother Keith (Malcolm Keen) a respected K.C. Keith is horrified at the damage this will do his career, but offers to help them escape while another suspect, a tramp, is tried for the murder. Larry insists on attending the trial, and when the tramp is found guilty he and Wanda commit suicide, leaving a note to exonerate him. In a bitter coda, Keith discovers the bodies and burns the note to save his own reputation.

In 1921 this was risky material. Even in 1937, when Dean filmed it with Laurence Olivier and Vivien Leigh, Graham Greene was forbidden to include the suicide and the miscarriage of British justice in his screenplay. He concocted a Greeneish story of redemption by a spoiled priest; the result was an unbalanced film where, as Roger Lewis points out, Olivier is playing Hamlet and Leigh shows no animation at all. 'There's no *enterprise* between Larry and Wanda,'[137] he complains. Between Albanesi and Nares there was precisely that. They were working on a short, almost skeletal text in which the emotional intensity never lets up but the performance styles change abruptly. They needed to develop a performance that indicated a past, a relationship and a social context for Larry and Wanda in a text that evaded the censor by operating through euphemisms, and in which most of the major events are narrated rather than staged. Wanda, for instance, has to pack virtually all her responses to her husband from his seduction when she is sixteen to his murder into the single line 'I see him now, always falling.'[138]

This densely packed realism had to harmonise with an ending that takes on a ritual element. There is firelight; Larry murmurs poetry as Wanda dresses in a robe and he arranges flowers around the table where they eat their last supper and drink their poisoned wine. Galsworthy's friend Schalit described Wanda's dramatic

---

[134] A.W.Pinero, *Trelawney of the Wells* (Heinemann1897), 213
[135] *Illustrated Sporting and Dramatic News*, June 1921
[136] *Pan,* June 1921
[137] Roger Lewis, *The Real Life of Laurence Olivier* (Century 1996), 146
[138] Galsworthy, *The First and the Last,* in *Six Short Plays* (Gerald Duckworth 1921), 25

4. With Lilian Braithwaite in *A Bill of Divorcement,* March 1921

journey in terms that suggest *Antony and Cleopatra.* 'Out of her first slavish devotion, she rises to the heights of sublime abnegation.'[139]

Cecil Chesterton's recollection of Meggie's performance suggests that she achieved this. 'There was that atmosphere of an emotional force which at any moment may become dynamic. The tense, quiet face, the haunted eyes, the tragic immobility of the husky voice, showed a sensibility which should have ripened into great art.'[140] Galsworthy was delighted. 'You go right to the heart,'[141] he wrote to her afterwards.

The reviews were full of praise for the actors, although there were reservations about the play. Meggie's tragic force was by now almost taken for granted: the real surprise for the critics was Nares. J.T. Grein, not a Galsworthy admirer, felt that the play had achieved something extraordinary. 'Besides the beautiful acting of Miss Meggie Albanesi, actress of temperament, of insight, of power, we discovered what we believed to be lurking in Mr Owen Nares. Here was no longer the darling of the gods, the charming young man of somewhat precious speech; here was a human being, suffering, shaken by emotion, true in all he had to convey. He may safely launch into Hamlet; he will succeed.'[142]

Nares was perhaps less Hamlet than Romeo; soliloquy was not really his style. His matinee idol typecasting was an inevitable consequence of his looks; the success he had made in his anodyne romantic roles was not. The play that made his reputation in middle age, *Robert's Wife* – in which he partnered Edith Evans to create an off-beat and believable marriage between a clergyman and a doctor with a mission to establish a family planning clinic – confirms an important aspect of his talent, a skill often undervalued: he was a brilliant doubles player. He was an actor who learned and grew through working with others, his charisma geared to establishing a relationship rather than a lone character on stage.

His autobiography pays generous tribute to his wife Marie Polini as mentor. However, she had her limits. Max Beerbohm once described her Goneril as 'wishing to show how charming and touching [she] too could be if [she] hadn't been cast for such unpleasant parts.'[143] Working with an actor of the calibre of Evans raised Nares's game; more opportunities of this kind might have brought him the reputation he deserved. Meggie always drew out fresh aspects of his talent, even when she was relatively inexperienced, even in drivel like *The Charm School.* She was now an established star. It was, perhaps, inevitable that they should begin an affair.

It was also inevitable that it would not last, but the end was brutal. After *The First and the Last* Nares continued toiling for Dean in the romantic mines with a play called *James the Less,* cast yet again as a man taking the blame for another's crime. This time most critics agreed he deserved something better than a play about 'being good-looking Owen Nares'.[144] The Aldwych venture collapsed, ReandeaN's finances being over-stretched, and Nares went on tour. In a scene straight from the previous century, Marie Polini discovered a letter from Meggie at the theatre. She ordered him to return it and inform Meggie that he would never see her alone again or accept any more letters.

---

[139] Leon Schalit, *John Galsworthy: A Survey* (Heinemann 1929),171
[140] *Sphere,* 22 Dec 1923
[141] *Meggie Albanesi*, 89
[142] *Illustrated London News,* 18 June 1921
[143] Max Beerbohm, *Last Theatres,* 486
[144] *Ladies Field,* 23 July 1921

ReandeaN programmes carried interviews with leading actors alongside the advertisements for corsets and chocolates. Nares had confided in a *Skin Game* programme that his motto was 'It's a long worm that has no turning.' This was evidently not a moment to turn and he obeyed Polini. Dean could barely forgive him; in his autobiography he excoriated Nares as 'always weak in [Polini's] hands'.[145] But one can hardly blame Polini, even if she was a lousy Goneril. As that rash of divorce plays demonstrated, divorce was not yet a realistic option for a wronged wife even if she wanted it. Nares was in any case devoted to his family. But Meggie was devastated, and there would continue to be consequences.

[145] Dean, *Seven Ages*, 147

‘Rush and whirl’

1922

‘Don’t be led into cheap stuff,’ John Galsworthy wrote to Meggie after seeing *A Bill of Divorcement*. ‘You have a great gift, and we want the utmost we can get from you on the English stage.’[146] As *Bill* continued its 1921 run he played cricket and wrote a new play with what seemed to him almost suspicious ease. He also reconsidered an old one. *Windows*, which he had written on a trip to America before the war, now seemed to him to contain a perfect part for Meggie Albanesi.[147] He offered it to Dean, who despite the success of *Bill* was still floundering financially after *Will Shakespeare* and the Aldwych experiments. Dean’s response was to ask for a look at the new play.

Windows was potentially a powerful opportunity for an actress of Meggie’s calibre and a company as politically aware as ReandeaN. A young woman is released after serving two years for infanticide and starts work as a maid to a rich family. The father is kindly but weak, the mother unforgiving and the rebellious son patronising: he kisses the girl for political rather than erotic reasons. She is already in love with a wastrel, and when finally disillusioned with him, she leaves, announcing ‘There’s nothing to be done with a girl like me.’[148] In an incongruous comic scene the family get drunk and discuss the nature of love; the action is interspersed with comments from the girl’s father, a philosophical window cleaner apparently on loan from Bernard Shaw.

It is clear what Galsworthy thought he had to offer Meggie. The role of Faith has Sydney’s cynical wit, the tragic sexuality of Wanda, and a capacity for sensual delight in all aspects of life, from chocolates to lighted streets, that calls for a stage presence of real vitality. Its chief power lies in a moment when Faith speaks about her vision of the baby’s future. ‘I didn’t want to kill it – I only wanted to save it from living,’[149] she tells the idealistic son of the house.

The scene is so unsparingly truthful that for one moment you catch a glimpse of a politically explosive drama with an extraordinary heroine, one with the insight and energy to challenge the standards of the society around her; Faith, followed to such a conclusion, would have given Meggie the kind of opportunity that *St Joan* gave Sybil Thorndike. However, this outburst vanishes into an unset dramaturgical jelly of social satire and feeble comedy and the implications of the baby’s death are forgotten. Galsworthy complained that ‘the philosophy [of the play] leaps so little to the minds of most folk,’[150] but outside the role of Faith the philosophy does not so much leap as mooch around in bedroom slippers; Dean’s instinct in rejecting

---

[146] *Meggie Albanesi,* 81
[147] J. Marriot, *The Life and Letters of John Galsworthy* (Heinemann 1935), 540
[148] John Galsworthy, *Windows,* Plays: Fifth Series (Duckworth and Co 1935), 98
[149] Galsworthy, *Windows* 55
[150] Marriot, *Life and Letters*, 540

Windows – despite the opportunity for Meggie to show the fiery political magic she had brought to *The Rising Sun* – was correct from both the dramaturgical point of view and that of the ReandeaN box office.

So was the instinct that led him to pester Galsworthy for the rights to the new play, of which Galsworthy himself said 'No management will refuse this.'[151] For it was *Loyalties,* his best and still his most famous play. Dean spotted a likely successor to *Bill of Divorcement.* Rehearsals began while critics were still urging the public to catch the final London performances of *Bill,* suggesting that they might conveniently include an outing to the St Martin's while in town to see the wedding of Princess Mary.[152] Archibald Haddon raised the stakes by asserting that *Bill* had changed the face of theatre: 'where are the dozens of cynical farces and decadent comedies and smutty revues, which recently disfigured the London stage? Vanished – or should we say banished – every one.'[153] *Loyalties* had the potential to meet this implicit challenge.

It could not have been more topical. Anti-Semitism emerged in Europe as a political force at the end of the previous century, a scapegoating reaction to the social changes of industrialisation. Hitler would write *Mein Kampf* the year after *Loyalties*. Galsworthy feared that the death of Edward VII, who had many Jewish friends, would revive a strain temporarily dormant in English society. The format of *Loyalties* also guaranteed success at the box-office: the whodunnit was the favourite middlebrow literary form of the period, and the play had a mystery, a court case with surprise witnesses and the upper-class perpetrator shooting himself offstage.

What it lacked was a good role for an actress. The dramatic honours were evenly divided between its leading men: Eric Maturin imbued Captain Dancy, thief and racist, with an athletic and dashing persona like his own: he was associated with the role all his life and brought similar charm to an innovative modern-dress Macbeth a few years later. Ernest Milton played De Levis, the abrasive Jewish social climber who moves from petulance at being robbed to fighting anti-Semitism. It was his first major West End role, one to which he had been drawn by his own Zionist sympathies.

Milton was a noted Old Vic performer, a glamorous and intelligent Hamlet, and although he expressed apprehension at the change of audience ('it's like being on trial for my life,' he told *Pall Mall,*[154]) he brought with him a fan base of intelligent and critical playgoers. A continuing interface between ReandeaN's modern focus and the developing classical tradition at the Vic might have proved enormously fruitful to both sides if ReandeaN had lasted into the next decade.

Meggie was cast as Dancy's naively loyal wife, 'poor little Mabel'. None of the female roles are rewarding – although Cathleen Nesbitt, a witty and politically aware performer, had some lines with bite – and Mabel is probably the least so. *Loyalties* is still absorbing in its sharp delineation of class and racial conflict; what dates it is the undiluted testosterone. Dancy and De Levis square up with sentiments like, 'So you shelter behind a woman, do you, you skulking cur!'[155] But the women remain unexasperated by these turkey-cock displays.

While it was clearly worthwhile to work on a play destined to be the theatrical talking point of 1922, Meggie expressed concern about her own input to

---

[151] Marriot, *Life and Letters,* 508
[152] *Sussex Daily News,* 7 Feb 1922
[153] *Sunday Express*, 5 March 1922
[154] *Pall Mall,* 11 March 1922
[155] Galsworthy, *Loyalties,* Five Plays (Methuen 1984), 373

5. With Eric Maturin in *Loyalties.* March 1922

Pall Mall: 'I am saying to myself… last time you had a fine part, which suited you to a miracle, a part full of opportunities, and the public liked you. Now you have a fine part, but not such an outstanding one. What have you done with it? Will the public say it was the part in *The Bill of Divorcement* [sic] that was fine, and not Meggie Albanesi?'[156] This was more than routine modesty for the press. Dean had found that even the vociferous reception of *Bill* could leave her in agonies of self-doubt. This time, the nature of the play meant that the response of the audience to her character would be muted and difficult to gauge.

It is a measure of the exhausting schedules inflicted on actors in the 1920s that Dean perceived *Loyalties* as under length and added a Barrie one-acter, *Shall We Join the Ladies?* Designed originally for an ADA gala, it is an acid little *jeu d'esprit,* which, like *Loyalties,* owes a lot to the whodunnit. All twelve guests summoned by a mysterious host have enough guilty secrets to make them suspects. All the original cast were established stars – Du Maurier had played the butler – so that there were no clues to be inferred from their status. The joke was that Barrie never bothered to reveal the murderer, concluding with a bloodcurdling offstage scream that could come from the killer or the next victim.

Dean retained the convention of all-star casting, borrowing Leslie Faber and Gladys Cooper (commuting across the West End from a play with an earlier curtain)

[156] *Pall Mall,* 11 March 1922

and Lady Tree. Meggie played Lady Jane. Tiny and venomous, she squared up to the enormously tall host – Dawson Millward, the upright colonel from *Loyalties* – before erupting into squeaks of fury as her fiancé ruined her alibi and returning his ring via the butler's tray. The comedy was all the sharper as an implicit parody of *Loyalties*, down to the casting of Eric Maturin as Meggie's beef-witted fiancé.

Dean managed the publicity for his double bill astutely. For the intellectuals there was lively press debate whether the censor should permit the word 'bloody': when he announced 'never in my lifetime', red-printed slips were inserted in the programmes to alert the audience to the omission.

For the more frivolous, there were press releases about the women's dresses to be specially imported from Paris. A fashion show was arranged at the St Martin's on the Sunday before the opening, with Meggie, Muriel Pratt and Cathleen Nesbitt modelling the Paris finery; but the plane ran into bad weather and they were left to entertain the journalists with tea and buns. Alec Rea's energetic American wife stood by at Croydon airport ready to fly out in a private plane and collect the dresses in person, but they managed to materialise in time for the first night. They were spectacularly stylish; Meggie as the youthful and serpentine Lady Jane found herself wearing 'silver brocaded tissue with a flounce of black Chantilly lace hanging over its knee-length train;'[157] it is a sexy and revealing garment, showing most of her legs through a transparent skirt, and in the production photographs she wears it with assurance.

Rehearsals were as exhausting as the chase for the costumes. Dean was even more testy than usual – Leslie Faber recalled getting a sympathetic pat from Meggie after a directorial tirade. Galsworthy hovered, having opted for a thermos at the dress rather than a PEN club dinner. He distributed Horlicks lozenges and whispered requests to the cast to underplay their lines – countermanded by Dean, which provoked one of the few rows between him and Galsworthy. Only Barrie remained cheerful, refusing to be drawn when every member of the cast badgered him to find out if he or she was playing the murderer. The dress rehearsal dragged on until eleven; this might have aroused fewer worries if Dean had not chosen this production to launch his policy of refusing to admit latecomers, an unprecedented step in the West End.

Loyalties was an instant success. The cast could have taken any number of curtain calls if they had not been too busy dressing for *Ladies*. Outside the box office the next morning the little stools that signified a willingness to queue for a day began to appear. Reviews were excellent, although some snide remarks vindicated Galsworthy's political pessimism: *Horse and Hound* sniffed it would get big audiences 'especially of the Chosen Race'[158] and another paper criticised the lack of 'realism' displayed by a Jew seeking to get into the Jockey Club, 'more exclusive than Boodles.'[159] In general the play was seen as outstanding , a fine piece of teamwork. The *Sunday Herald* considered it 'a play that makes the carping critic want to go home and put his head in the gas oven – his occupation is gone.'[160] ReandeaN's radical credentials were confirmed. *The Athenaeum* felt that the upper class had received a double lambasting, 'denounced for a gang of he and she Borgias,' and disapproved of the comedy in *Ladies,* complaining 'some people would laugh at the Day of Judgement.'[161]

---

[157] 'Long-Skirted and Lovely: The Ladies of *Shall We Join the Ladies?* at the St. Martin's', *Sketch,* 15 March 1922
[158] *Horse and Hound*, 11 March 1922
[159] *Winning Post*, 18 March 1922
[160] *Sunday Herald*, 12 March 1922
[161] *Athenaeum,* 11 March 1922

6. Double Bill: with Eric Maturin and Leslie Faber in
Shall We Join the Ladies,. March 1922

Despite her fears, Meggie's performance was generally praised, the only dissenter being Christopher St John who found it 'fussy' and 'noisy', although suggesting that this might have been Dean's fault.[162] For most critics Meggie seemed natural and unforced, and several sympathised with the women in the cast for 'having to pretend that they matter.'[163] A lively argument arose in *The Star* when

[162] *Time and Tide*, 24 March 1922
[163] *Illustrated Sporting and Dramatic News,* 18 March 1922

'Gallery Girl' deprecated the male assumption that Dancy's suicide was the Decent Thing to do; she pointed out that no woman would want her husband to shoot himself to shield her from disgrace.[164] This may indicate something of Meggie's approach to the role; one photograph of Maturin and Milton in turkey-cock mode shows her restrained as Mabel, cooling the emotional temperature rather than raising it by frenzied reactions.

Some reviews, however, used generalised superlatives she might have found unhelpful. When they state she was the only performer 'getting exactly the right effect of conversational speech'[165] or that 'short as her part was, Meggie Albanesi gave a performance that could not be equalled among the men,'[166] they seem to be moving away from judging a particular performance to confirming a decision about her star status already made. She was painfully aware of the fragility of such status: several contemporaries remarked that she would never criticise another performer or allow those closest to her, like Effie, to compare her with others to their hurt. And for the foreseeable future she was working at an unrewarding but extremely demanding schedule: as soon as the queues formed Dean laid on extra matinees, and the lengthy bill played for eight, nine or even ten times a week.

There were a few diversions. The abortive fashion show led to some opportunities to model for Florence Vandamm, who would soon move to New York and become the most famous photographer on Broadway. Her pictures in *Vogue* and *Draper's Organiser.*[167] show Meggie in a variety of modern dresses (including something called a 'race gown'). In all of them she looks slightly awkward, a young woman doing her best to find an animated pose, but not at home in front of the camera. They are a marked contrast to her production photographs, which never betray self-consciousness even in formalised foyer portraits when she is only partly in character. Being herself was difficult at the best of times. After the breakup with Nares, it seems to have been very difficult indeed and her hectic lifestyle was beginning to cause her friends serious concern.

New nightclubs were opening every day. It was fashionable to tut-tut about ' youth', and 'youth' increasingly used the clubs as a space in which to act out a new social and sexual identity. The Shimmy and the Twinkle, lively but innocuous, gave way to dances with more intimate body contact; you could glue yourself to your partner and foxtrot in a tightly confined space the whole night. Writers like Meggie's friend Michael Arlen offered the young a modern and romantic self-image, courageous, truth telling, wild and doomed. Celebrity hunting was as much part of the club adventure as cocktails. Arlen himself could be found at the more upmarket venues looking glamorous. His motto, he used to say, was *per ardua ad astrakhan*.

But he understood that *ardua* required sleep, food and quiet. Most of those who successfully defined twenties youth to itself were careful to be seen in the right places with the right look, but had no intention of acting out the self-destructive image to the bitter end. Noel Coward still lived with his mother. Of those who *did* all the things Coward and Arlen wrote about, some did not need to earn a living and some were severely damaged by their failure to balance life and work. The London theatre was haunted by the death at the Victory Ball of drug-addicted starlet Billie

---

164 'A Gallery Girl Writes', *Star*, 15 March 1922
165 *Athenaeum*, 18 March 1922
166 *Brighton Standard*, 16 March 1922
167 *Vogue*, April 1922; *Draper's Organiser*, 15 April 1922

Carleton, the inspiration of several plays including *The Vortex*. Tallulah Bankhead, the sexiest star of all, could be spectacularly brilliant, but drugs, drink and lovers made her increasingly unreliable and she never lived up to her potential.

Meggie fitted into neither group. She worked furiously, reluctant to miss a performance even when ill; her passion was rehearsal, where she could experiment freely, and she was, as Dean observed in his obituary, the first to arrive and the last to leave. 'Sometimes,' he recorded, 'she almost had to be driven away.'[168] But increasingly she danced all night and almost never went home alone.

One person greatly worried by this was the Shrimp. Fabia Drake had finally left RADA and at seventeen launched herself on the London theatre while *Bill* was at the height of its success. During the inevitable period of rejections she cheered herself up by visiting Meggie in her offstage waits. Given the strain Meggie experienced playing Sydney it is a measure of her affection for the Shrimp that Drake found her unfailingly kind, 'a lodestar in my bleak night sky'.[169]

But Drake found herself disconcerted by Meggie's post-theatre lifestyle: once she had wiped off Sydney's make-up she would walk over to Ciro's in Orange Street and sit at her table on the balcony until she picked up a man for the night. If this troubled Drake, it also seemed to trouble Meggie herself. 'You can never understand,' she told her, 'the postman will do.' Drake perceived her as the victim of a cruel trick of nature:

> I was to learn during these visits to someone who seemed to have the world at her feet how strangely difficult her own life had become; for she was of that rare and fated genus, she was a true, and seemingly helpless, nymphomaniac…this beloved girl – no one who ever played with her failed to love her – was stricken with an awful disease.[170]

Drake was devoutly religious and struggling to come to terms with the behaviour of a friend she loved too much to condemn. Basil Dean, more prosaic and more optimistic, thought that Meggie was merely trying to blot out the pain of her break with Nares.

It is worth remembering, however, that everyone who danced at the nightclubs in the twenties had a smattering of popular psychology. People talked airily of complexes and repressions, of Freud and Havelock Ellis and Krafft-Ebing; it is possible Meggie applied Drake's label to herself. Arlen's 1924 bestseller *The Green Hat* explored the idea of nymphomania in relation to a cynical heroine as emblematic of the twenties as Sydney, a woman who 'destroys her body because she must'.[171] The mixture of emotional loss, Catholic guilt and lack of confidence in her own talent could have made it hard to believe that the memory of Nares would fade, that there would be better roles in which she could express her times rather than living out their strains in her own body. The term that fits her best, perhaps, sits in the dictionary just prior to the over-abused 'nymphomania': 'Nympholepsy, n. Ecstasy or frenzy caused by desire of the unattainable.'

She could not help knowing that what she wanted was not the sex and the dancing; what they gave her was the chance to go on with the process of giving

---

[168] Meggie Albanesi Scholarship Matinee programme, Basil Dean Archive.
[169] Fabia Drake, *Blind Fortune* (William Kimber 1978), 45
[170] Drake, *Blind Fortune*, 45
[171] Michael Arlen, *The Green Hat (* Collins 1924), 47

bodily expression to her feelings, an extension of the rehearsal process where no line has to be drawn under the performer's accomplishment. It was when she stopped to reflect, that moment when the curtain came down, that she was most unhappy, never convinced that she had given enough despite every assurance to the contrary.

There were, meanwhile, friends who tried to make things easier. She had secretarial help from her cousin May Hallatt and from Lorn Macnaughtan, a friend of Betty Chester to whom she became particularly close. Lorn, about five years her senior, came from a rather grand Scottish family who had fallen on hard times; she earned a perilous living as a chorus girl, although, as Noel Coward unkindly put it, 'she appeared to have no attributes whatever for that particular sphere. Her feet were large and her figure unvoluptuous; she could neither dance nor sing.'[172] Lorn opted instead to act as secretary to Effie and Meggie, and would finally run Coward's life for forty-six years, coping with widowhood and children as she did so. The ironical, efficient Monica who looks after Gary Essendine in *Present Laughter* is a portrait of her. Lorn wrote her own tribute to herself:

> E Maria Albanesi
> Thinks I am a perfect daisy.[173]

Lorn's kindly cynicism did nothing to persuade Meggie to rest. Nor did Effie's tight-lipped determination to utter no reproaches (although Meggie, a child of her generation, protected her parents from anything she considered too shocking for them, refusing to lend Effie her copy of *Ulysses*). But the dancing, the lovers and the demands of the double bill were taking a toll of her health.

In June there was an opportunity that might have boosted her confidence as an actress. Hitherto her only films had been versions of stage plays and she had not especially enjoyed them; her own taste ran more to the Hollywood Westerns she liked to watch with Effie. Victor Sjöstrom was an international name, a major force in the emerging Swedish film industry: his best pictures were noted for social realism and a radiantly beautiful treatment of the Scandinavian landscape, and many featured powerful roles for women.

Unfortunately Sjöstrom was being pressured to make action movies to compete in the American market. *Det Omringade Huset* (*Surrounded House,* released in the UK as *Honour*) was one of these. The plot derived from a play by Pierre Frondaie, itself highly derivative: an English Lieutenant renounces his commission and his fiancée because of his father's gambling debts ; he pays them off and returns to the regiment only to find that she has married the colonel. He does his best to die heroically fighting the Bedouin, is mistaken for a spy and nearly shot; however, the colonel saves his life and gives the couple his blessing before he obligingly dies and leaves them free to marry. Sjöstrom felt 'fed up and depressed'[174] at the prospect. The budget forced him to shoot the Bedouin scenes in Ekero, where extras from the Swedish Army charged glumly across windswept Scandinavian dunes, shivering in khaki shorts and trying to look British.

Meggie found filming with Sjöstrom a happy experience and was feted throughout her five-week stay in the 'cinema town' Svensk Filmindustri had created

[172] Noel Coward, *Present Indicative* (Methuen 1999), 77
[173] Cole Lesley , *Noel Coward and His Friends* (Weidenfeld and Nicolson 1979), 72
[174] Bengt Forslund, *Victor Sjöstrom,* tr. P. Cowie (Zoetrope NY 1988), quoting Sjöstrom's letter to Hjalmar Bergman, 7 July 1922

outside Stockholm. She was reunited with Matheson Lang from *Mr Wu*, and took to her Swedish co-stars, her fluent German bridging any gaps in their English. She made plans to visit the following year. The British Legation threw a dinner party for the Crown Prince of Denmark, to which she was invited, the British Press describing her as 'one of the most admired beauties'.[175] She never saw the finished film, which was released after her death; it was not a critical success, nor did it achieve its aim of breaking into the US market. Sjöstrom subsequently suppressed as many copies as possible, and the experience helped him make up his mind to go and work for Sam Goldwyn in Hollywood.

This was no reflection on his stars: the remaining stills of more intimate moments suggest thoughtful and restrained work (though the makeup for the Bedouins is beyond redemption). The potent and unusual mix of Meggie and Sjöstrom might have eventually surfaced in a better vehicle ; if she, like him, had survived to work with Ingmar Bergman, there might have been a celluloid record to match her stage work.

The break in Sweden did restore her to health and energy; she returned in July to do eight performances a week as Mabel Dancy, but Dean also had a new project, which he had been publicising since June. George Grossmith and J.A.E. Malone had taken over His Majesty's, in eclipse since the death of Beerbohm Tree, and wanted a production to put it back on the map. Dean was invited to produce the new Somerset Maugham play *East of Suez.* The offer signified real recognition of his own achievements and those of ReandeaN. Dean, Rea and George Harris had celebrated the success of *Loyalties* with a tour of Europe to study technical innovations and this would allow them to try out spectacular effects on a budget way beyond that of the St Martin's. Harris could stage the Great Gate of Peking, a Chinese temple, and a street complete with a real Ford Model T; the opening allowed Dean to commission special music and to marshal forty-odd Chinese extras as well as a mix of West End stars and ReandeaN performers, including founder members Meggie and Malcolm Keen.

The stakes were high: Dean had dogsbodied for Tree in the cavernous playhouse and felt that as a 'provincial newcomer' he was being challenged to fill Tree's shoes. He was already overworked and strained and rehearsals did little to reassure him. Maugham was an unenthusiastic presence. He and Dean had a brief spat over props: asked by the stage manager what sort of sandwiches he should provide for an afternoon tea scene, Dean suggested cucumber. Maugham spluttered into malevolent life to snap that this was ridiculous. Dean recalled wishing the grave trap would open and swallow him up;[176] the niceties of colonial etiquette evidently made him feel like a provincial hick. He took it out on Henry Kendall, cast as the punctilious Englishman who warns his friend against marrying a half-Chinese girl; so unpleasant was he that Maugham sparked briefly into life again with a cutting remark about Dean 'burning the Kendall at both ends'.

During *East of Suez* Meggie was seriously depressed. She told Effie that she felt miscast, too young for the role; she was terrified of failure and her previous successes did not encourage her. Ian Holm describes this terror as an inevitable accompaniment of unrepeatable performances like Olivier's peak Othello:

---

[175] *Daily Graphic,* 17 July 1922

[176] MS of Dean's volume for the Geoffrey Bles series *Play Production,* 1929, Basil Dean Archive DEA12/1/62

> Olivier knew he was good – knew he was often brilliant – but rarely was he so good that his lack of control (his say) in the matter was exposed. And if he didn't have control, how could he be certain that one day he wouldn't be as bad as that night his Othello had been good?[177]

The nerves manifested themselves in a sore throat, which by the dress rehearsal stage left her almost unable to speak. Sybil Thorndike took care of her, slipping over from the New where she was appearing in *Scandal* to nurse her, but in the event Norah Robinson, her understudy, appeared at the dress and Meggie played the first night with a new-fangled 'electric treatment' applied to her throat every time she came offstage. Dean was almost too exhausted to comfort her.

The problem was not that she was miscast, nor did it lie in Dean's direction. It lay in the play itself. *The Spectator* imagined a conversation between Dean and Maugham:

> 'Those Chinese fellows, down at Limehouse, you know? Couldn't we get a lot of them to walk on? You could put in something about opium and joss-sticks…and how about pidgin English – 'Me no savvy – you catchee top-side?'And don't you think Miss Meggie Albanesi ought to have a really strong part….how long would you want to do us a play like that?' And one imagines Mr Maugham replying, 'A fortnight.'And perhaps in answer to a raised eyebrow reducing it to two days.[178]

The acid review is unfair to Dean – this was an offer he could not refuse – but it catches both the technical and moral difficulties of the play. Despite the realistic street scenes, it is really an attempt to graft a fashionable Chinoiserie onto Edwardian society drama – *The Second Mrs Tanqueray Meets Chu Chin Chow* – and there are problems with both aspects.

East of Suez leaves an unpleasant taste in the mouth, but it is necessary to unpack the nature of its racism in context. Plays with sinister oriental villains and titles like *Yellow Snare* were common in the 1920s: the censor considered these might be offensive to Chinese people, but did not see that as a reason to ban them. He did, however, consider that the subject of interracial marriage might constitute such a reason. He passed *East of Suez* because 'the character of the half-caste, Daisy, is vile and evil and the presentment of her a sort of wholesome warning.'[179] He was by no means alone in his attitude and it is worth noting that even Clemence Dane was not above exploiting it in her thriller *Enter Sir John*.[180]

Maugham's play contains some self-consciously liberal remarks against 'colour prejudice'. However, the Chinese characters comprise a mother who pimps her mixed-race daughter Daisy, Lee Tai, a gangster, who buys Daisy, and Daisy herself, who connives at the attempted murder of her English husband and sleeps with his best friend. Her sexuality is perceived as something almost vampiric and inextricable from her origins. At one point she puts on an elaborate Manchu dress, and her dreary husband gasps:

---

[177] Ian Holm/Steve Jacobi, *Acting My Life* (Bantam 2004),142–3
[178] *Spectator*, 9 Sept 1922
[179] Steve Nicolson, *The Censorship of British Drama 1900–1968,* Vol. I (University of Exeter Press 2002) , 285
[180] Filmed in 1930 by Alfred Hitchcock as *Murder!* from the play by Clemence Dane and Helen Simpson

> You've brought all the East into the room with you. My head reels as though I were drunk ….I thought that no one in the world was more normal than I. I'm ashamed of myself. You're almost a stranger to me, and by God, I feel as though the marrow of my bones were melting. I hear the East a-calling….[181]

This is the Daisy who at the final curtain reveals how 'evil' she is by donning the dress again and painting her face to suit it. Maugham's stage direction reads '*she looks on a sudden absolutely Chinese.*'[182] Any actress might be forgiven for not fulfilling that to the letter. However, the difficulty was exacerbated by the fact that the text contains another Daisy altogether.

Agate had noted that in terms of sexual politics the drama 'was to stray no farther than Streatham'.[183] It was full of stale Pinero devices: compromising letters, a woman with a past, tattling neighbours wondering if a so-called 'widow' has ever been married, former lovers turning up at inconvenient moments, a repentant adulterer who shoots himself 'in deference to the *convenances*'.[184] But by 1922 about one young woman in three had a 'past', or at least some sexual experience and *Bill* had put divorce on the theatrical map.

By 1924 Coward would deconstruct the Edwardian conventions; in *Easy Virtue* he explored the old situation of a divorced woman coolly received by society, but located the motive for such ostracism not in moral scruples but (bang up to Freudian date) sexual repression. Daisy's situation had the potential for a more complex reception before an audience where young iconoclasts mixed with old Edwardians.

However, whether the actor chose to interpret Daisy through the moral lens of old fashioned society drama or through modernist rejection of all it stood for, the combination of her human story with crude racial politics typing her as straightforwardly 'evil' was never going to make for psychological coherence. It is no wonder Meggie felt unequal to it. The reviews for her performance, as for the play as a whole, were mixed. But if favourable and disparaging comments are read side by side, what does emerge is the image of a performance produced through a series of careful choices.

The most apparently successful of these involved the way she showed the emotional make-up of Daisy. The *Illustrated London News* praised her ability 'to tackle successfully and convincingly the storms of emotion through which she passes, [a] plain enough indication of how far in art and temperament she out-tops most of the young actresses who are her contemporaries.'[185] George Arliss wrote to her that 'you achieved what I should have believed to be impossible if I had read the play. You created in our heart a great sympathy for Daisy.'[186]

Photographs suggest that she did not achieve this by sentimentalising the character. In one, she is shaking her mother viciously, stressing the height that makes her different, more European than the old lady. (Meggie was small: this is an effect she and Marie Ault must have worked hard for.) In another she has her hands round the throat of Lee Tai, her face twisted with rage. Nor did she shirk Daisy's

---

[181] Somerset Maugham, *East of Suez,* Collected Plays Vol. 3 (Heinemann 1961),150
[182] Maugham, *East of Suez*, 219
[183] *Saturday Review,* 17 Sept 1922
[184] *Saturday Review,* 17 Sept 1922
[185] *Illustrated London News,* 9 Sept 1922
[186] *Meggie Albanesi*, 107

manipulative side. At the end of the fifth scene Daisy collapses and is carried off by her ex-lover George; the ironic grunt of her corrupt old mother suggests that this collapse is staged. Photographs show Meggie's swoon as transparently fake, her eyes open and fixed on the fleeing George; when he lifts her she makes an ugly lump in his arms, too tense to be genuinely unconscious.

It is interesting to follow her eyes in the production photographs: they suggest that a keynote of her performance was watchfulness. This is a person of intelligence, capable of judging others. While other characters make eye contact or admire the scenery Daisy is always looking intently at someone not looking at her. This nudges the spectator into adopting her point of view, or at least paying close attention to her very visible subtext. She frequently makes small gestures that cannot be observed by the other characters. Her feelings about Sylvia, the English girl who patronises her while falling in love with George, are made clear without a word. As the men cluster like a bunch of flowers around the figure described by Maugham as 'so springlike and fresh that it is a pleasure to look at her',[187] Daisy watches expressionlessly, but her hands clench in her lap.

The mother is given speeches in pidgin that were played for laughs and won excellent notices for Marie Ault. When Meggie's Daisy watches her there is a look of contempt on her face that is invisible to everyone else; it seems to be passing judgement not only on her mother's treatment of her but on the way she acts out her racial stereotype for the entertainment of Westerners. Later an identical expression crosses her face when she looks at her husband, equally stereotypical in the prejudices that bar him from understanding her.

Throughout, Daisy's behaviour is immoral but never unmotivated. The 'sympathy' that Arliss perceived suggests that she revealed the connections between Daisy's corruption and her past, betrayed by George and commodified by her mother and Lee Tai. The search for motivation may have underlain Meggie's complaint to her mother that she was 'too young' to get Daisy right in all the details; but she made sense of her.

What she did not do was to integrate the melodramatic vamp, and the negative comments on her performance are those that regret its absence. The *Spectator* considered that the actors were 'unconvinced' and that Meggie 'looked beautiful, though never for one moment the hard, exotic sensualist she should have been'.[188] John Gielgud concurred. 'She lacks allurement,'[189] he noted on his programme with the pomposity of his eighteen years.

That bone-melting, East a-calling stuff, however, is not a quality that can be shown from within: it inheres in the reactions of the observers. The best Cleopatras do wit and passion and let the poetry of the smitten observers take care of the allure. Meggie could be sexually magnetic onstage, but the only way to convey the irresistible evil George and Henry see in her would be to 'impersonate' a stereotype. She was never going to succeed as long as she grounded her performance in psychological realism.

It may be that the use of her Italian looks in the service of a crudely generalised 'foreignness' irritated her. In Hollywood Rudolph Valentino was expressing resentment at being 'obliged to play like an emotional Italian'[190] with a

[187] Maugham, *East of Suez,* 167
[188] *Spectator,* 9 Sept 1922
[189] *John Gielgud's Notes from the Gods,* ed. R. Mangan (NHB 1994) , *East of Suez* programme
[190] Emily W. Leider, *Dark Lover: the Life and Death of Rudolph Valentino* (Faber and Faber 2003), 172

7. L to R: Henry Kendall, Malcolm Keen, Meggie Albanesi and Marie Ault in *East of Suez,* September 1922

lot of 'eye-rolling', whether he was cast as a Sheik, a Russian, or an Argentinian. Even Effie seemed to talk about 'the Latin temperament'[191] as if it made Meggie a kind of exotic alien. Photographs of the production show the Chinese characters in extraordinarily unconvincing make-up, something that might have come from *Yellow Snare.* You wonder – as James Agate did at the time – what the forty Chinese extras made of it all.

The decision not to conform to the stereotype and be 'alluring' may have been conscious or unconscious, but it brought to the performance the same sexual honesty that had desentimentalised Elise in *The Charm School.* Agate felt that she lacked power in *East of Suez,* but not truth. 'She forced her essential rightness and singleness of purpose to shine through…hammered some spark of nobility out of her material, however unpromising.[192]

Photographed by the *Sketch* at this point for a series about the hands of popular actresses, she seemed to make this point visually. While others in the series opted for old-fashioned gestures that allowed them to import an emotional content (Madge Titherage, old enough to know better, sucks a finger with a revolting childish simper) Meggie lit a cigarette, put on a ring, and studiously avoided cliché; the result gives the sense of an actor at work rather than posing as an object of consumption.[193]

[191] *Meggie Albanesi*, 69
[192] James Agate, *The Times,* 16 Dec 1923
[193] *Sketch,* 6 Dec 1922

This honesty brought power to the one moment even her most disparaging critics admired: the speech in which Daisy tries to persuade George to smoke opium. It stands apart from the rest of the play. It can seem like an irrelevance, like the Chinese wedding procession Maugham imported for gratuitous local colour. For Noel Coward, it was, as he wrote to her after the first night, a fit conclusion to 'the best thing that anyone has done for years…exquisite and damnably difficult. I'm very, very proud of you.'[194] For Gielgud it was 'perfect'[195] .

The speech is not so much an account of an opium vision as an opportunity for Daisy to declare her love for George and hypnotise him into loving her. For Meggie it was a chance to beckon her audience:

> After you've smoked a pipe or two your mind grows extraordinarily clear. You have a strange facility of speech and yet no desire to speak. All the puzzles of this puzzling world grow plain to you. You are tranquil and free. Your soul is released from the bondage of your body and it plays happy and careless like a child with flowers. Death cannot frighten you and want and misery are like blue mountains far away. You feel a heavenly power possess you and you can venture all things because suffering cannot touch you. Your spirit has wings and you fly like a bird through the starry wastes of the night. You hold space and time in the hollow of your hand. Then you come upon the dawn, all pearly and grey and silent, and there in the distance like a dreamless sleep is the sea.[196]

W.G. Royde-Smith said of her that in any play all her previous parts 'marched behind the current character to round out her conception'.[197] This is not a remark about characterisation – her roles were never alike – but about theatricality, a relationship with the audience that grew and developed. What they wanted from her was not just to see a character in the round, but to have an experience she gave them directly and which, increasingly, they trusted her to give. Dean spoke of a point when acting becomes 'almost impersonal…[it] presents human emotion – abstract, glorified, almost religious.'[198] The opium speech is about the power of illusion from the point of view of one both subject to it and exercising it; over and above anything Daisy feels it makes the audience understand what the actor is offering if they follow when she beckons.

It is also, of course, a speech about addiction; and she understood addiction, although for her it was not to drugs. But the essential dishonesty of the play made it a problem, for her co-stars as well. She felt she ought to solve it and never could. Her health continued to suffer and Norah Robinson played for two or three days of the first week. The next five months saw her still struggling. Effie thought that her failure to make the dress rehearsal – to which the influential Sunday press were invited – made her feel she had let the company down and soured the role for her.

The box office receipts were respectable, though, and the image of Meggie in the Manchu dress seemed to catch the public imagination. Her photograph was used to advertise the Boxing Day fancy dress ball at the Belgravia, where she judged

---

[194] *Meggie Albanesi,* 106–7
[195] Gielgud, *East of Suez* programme
[196] Maugham, *East of Suez,* 106
[197] *The Weekly Westminster,* 15 Dec 1923
[198] Programme, Meggie Albanesi scholarship matinee

costumes alongside Isabel Jeans. But *East of Suez* not only failed to boost her self-confidence, it seemed to wreck it altogether. Barbara Cartland remembered her weeping with frustration in the dressing room.[199]

Interviewed between performances by a reporter from *Royal Magazine* Meggie talked about the 'rush and whirl' of work and said that she found acting harder, not easier, as she went on. She dwelt again on professional insecurity. 'If the part comes to you, you must stick to it, whatever happens – they can always find someone else to replace you tomorrow.' The early 1920s had seen an epidemic of short runs and tiny houses (one two thousand-seater playhouse had notoriously drawn an audience of six) and the *Express* estimated that only six of the forty West End theatres were breaking even.[200]

ReandeaN had been remarkably successful in weathering financial storms, but nothing could be taken for granted. However, she was failing to acknowledge her own status within the company; Dean saw her as a leader as well as a box office draw. She had no tips for success: she attributed her own to 'luck – heaps of luck'. She seemed not so much in love with the theatre as addicted, expressing a longing to 'sail out somewhere – anywhere ….but if I ever do I shall take the first boat back.'[201] By the time the interview was published she had sailed out: Dean recognised that she could not go on in her state of health and she embarked to visit Eva in NewYork.

[199] Barbara Cartland, *We Danced All Night* (Robson Books 1994), 141
[200] W. Macqueen-Pope, *The Footlights Flickered* (Herbert Jenkins1959), 69
[201] *Royal Magazine*, Feb 1923.

‘St Martin’s for progress’
1924

The plan was for Meggie to take a short break while the company got on with a new play by A.A. Milne at the St Martin’s and *East of Suez* finished its run at His Majesty’s. Dean was optimistic about ReandeaN. They had a new state-of-the-art lighting system from Dresden, financed by Rea. They created an in-house magazine to replace programmes. Edited by the dynamic publicity officer, the left-wing poet W.R. Titterton, it worked on several levels to construct a company identity; there were snippets of backstage gossip and serious articles which explored the repertoire in relation to wider debates.

Plans were also moving ahead for a series of special matinees called the Playbox. Unlike the Aldwych experiments these would be mounted in-house, with the possibility of extending a successful production. They were financed by a subscription system – a strategy that was not only shrewd business but suggested to the audience that they were partners in the ReandeaN enterprise. Along with established figures like Maugham and Barrie, new playwrights such as Dane, Miles Malleson and Coward had plays scheduled for Playbox; the point was to challenge and develop performers and public alike. Velona Pilcher, an expressionist playwright, declared her hope that the mix of talents would produce non-naturalistic work as distinguished as the company’s social-realistic drama. ‘St. Martin’s for progress and ReandeaN to the rescue!’[202] she proclaimed in *Time and Tide.*

Several projects were planned around Meggie. Clemence Dane had written *The Way Things Happen,* the most explicitly feminist play that had so far emerged from ReandeaN, specifically for her. *The Lilies of the Field,* by a young playwright already successful in revue, John Hastings Turner, was chosen to give her a chance to play light comedy. Despite all Meggie’s apprehensions about finding herself out of work, Dean considered she ‘had become a pivotal figure in my forward planning’,[203] an inextricable part of the ReandeaN identity.

The plans were thrown into disarray – first by the failure of the Milne play and then by Meggie’s late return. The break must have done little to alleviate her exhaustion. The atmosphere at the Curtis Brown farm near Binghampton in upstate New York – a Spartan place currently home to Marshall, Eva, their three daughters and one of Marshall’s more difficult uncles – was extremely strained. Eva’s relationship with the semi-invalid Marshall was disintegrating. Meggie’s stay was punctuated by severe headaches and there were times when she was too ill to leave the house. Neither Meggie nor Eva communicated much of this to Effie. Eva sent cheerful party anecdotes and described Meggie larking about with a friend’s top hat over the austere chignon she had retained from *East of Suez.* When Meggie returned

---

[202] *Time and Tide*, 23 March 1923
[203] Dean, *Seven Ages*, 191

8. As Daisy in *East of Suez,* September 1922

on the *Majestic* in March, however, much later than anticipated, she had to be carried off the boat and went almost directly into a nursing home.

The story for the press was that she had caught a bad cold and had unwisely gone for a swim in the ship's pool. In her biography of Meggie Effie mentions an operation for appendicitis. But that was not the whole story; it is evident from her painful reticence that Effie was ignorant or unwilling to write it all. She speaks vaguely of 'grave illness' and about an operation later in the year that was 'as it were, a second edition of the first one'.[204] The illness was peritonitis, which renders the whole system inflamed and toxic. It can have a number of causes, but it is clear that at some point there had been an abortion which had gone wrong. Dean was inclined to think that this might have happened more than once, though he judged this not from direct knowledge but from the last doctor's description of the damage done to her.

Dean protected Effie from this information just as her daughter did. Few of Meggie's theatre contemporaries would have been judgemental. Some were blasé – Lorn Macnaughtan liked to quote one of her fellow chorus girls on a friend in the same predicament, 'Silly girl, fancy letting him put it there!'[205] Bankhead in extravagant moments boasted that the Prince of Wales had donated a pint of blood for her own operation. But information in the world before the Abortion Act circulated in a mix of bravado and fear. There were no guarantees of safety. Wealth and education did not protect women from danger: a friend of Michael Arlen in a politically sensitive relationship was sent to Paris as the safest option and died of peritonitis.

Meggie's heritage made things even harder. She was a cradle Catholic; she took this seriously enough to attach herself to the Catholic Actors' Guild and abortion was not something she could have undertaken lightly. She also adored her Catholic father and the family way was to protect him from as many crises as possible: one of her first acts after establishing herself in the nursing home was to send a note to his hotel telling him, 'I am quite happy about everything except you. I don't want you to fret, darling.'[206] At best, she had spent the last few months in a state of guilt and worry and put her own safety low on the list of priorities: at worst, the self-destructive streak may have led her to ignore it deliberately. Her mental and physical state must have been appallingly fragile.

The operation appeared successful, but in the days before antibiotics there was serious risk of infection. In two days she was considered to be out of danger, but was extremely depressed. Alec Rea's wife carried her off to their house in the country as soon as she could be moved. After three weeks she went to Folkestone and the press ran cheerful stories about her convalescence; there were photographs of her astride a small pony belonging to friends and the story of her unlucky swim made light of her illness.

Dean had kept the St Martin's afloat by a hastily organised production of Capek's *R.U.R.* This became a cult success; ex-servicemen hawking models of the robots designed by George Harris outside the theatre did excellent business. However, the postponed production meant that the St Martin's was dark for a fortnight and the actors unpaid for the first time in ReandeaN's history. *The Lilies of the Field,* already advertised in the news sheet, went into rehearsal in early May, accompanied by a flurry of good wishes for Meggie's health in the press; it was set to run alongside *R.U.R.* at the St Martin's sister theatre, the almost equally intimate and attractive Ambassadors.

Relations between Meggie and Dean were strained. Apparently unaware of the difficulties of her time with Eva he attributed Meggie's collapse to 'an over-

---

[204] *Meggie Albanesi*, 178
[205] Philip Hoare, *Noel Coward* (Sinclair-Stevenson 1995), 79
[206] *Meggie Albanesi*,125

enthusiastic welcome on Broadway,'[207] and she had too much sense of responsibility to the company to take a longer break. She resumed a hectic nightclub life: she was spotted at Ciro's and was a Thursday regular at the Embassy on Bond Street, what the Prince of Wales called 'the Buckingham Palace of nightclubs', where your status was measured not by what you wore or ate but in how the cloakroom attendant and the old man selling flowers at the gate greeted you. Dean, like most of her friends, remonstrated with her about the need to slow down, rest, and take fewer risks.

He was probably less well equipped to do so than most. His account of his own relationships at this time, written in 1970, would sound a note of Pooterish comedy if they were not so painfully honest. Raw from the break-up of his marriage, he squired her about for a while, convinced that his feelings were Platonic. The tone of his reminiscences suggests that he was deceiving himself. 'She preferred gay partners, comedians and jockeys. How I hated those raffish friends! None of them seemed to appreciate the precious jewel of her friendship…I raged inwardly.'[208]

While Dean was probably familiar with the shifting meaning of the word 'gay', it seems to be used here in the wistful sense of 'more fun than I was'. And there is incomprehension as well as wounded feelings in that phrase 'comedians and jockeys'. While, like Meggie, they used the clubs to unwind (that year the exuberant Steve Donaghue danced at three London night spots in succession only hours after winning his third successive Derby), it seems perverse of Dean to direct his scorn at two of the most disciplined professions on earth. They shared with her an understanding of what it was like to face an audience, what it was like to nerve up your body in the face of exhaustion and injury. Perhaps, after all, Meggie did not choose her partners as blindly as she thought: the postman would not do. Dean's sermons failed; he went dancing instead with Nancie Parsons, cast as the parlourmaid in *Lilies,* and eventually married her; when he encountered Meggie at nightclubs, they had corrosive rows.

Meanwhile, they were working on their light comedy. Meggie played one of a vicar's twin daughters, set by their grandmother to compete for the same man with a month in London as the prize. Edna Best, as the prettier sister, tries to vamp him with the flapper's entire armoury; the clever sister, aware that he is obsessed with Victorian values, dons sausage curls and a hoop skirt and simpers, 'For a long time I have felt that the modern girl is not modest enough.'[209] Naturally he falls for her, and she for him. In London she sparks off a cult for crinolines but increasingly worries that she will lose him when the truth emerges. She doesn't, of course, as he has already seen her jazzing quietly to herself, and the play ends with him watching adoringly as she enters, 'the minx of 1923', in a dazzling low cut dress way beyond the budget of a vicar's daughter.

Featherweight it might be, but *Lilies* was highly topical. The *Brideshead* generation obsessively collected wax fruit, stuffed birds and fragments of Victoriana. Harold Acton wore the clothes of a 1840s dandy. When Lytton Strachey's biography of Victoria was published in 1921 the Oxford Aesthetes planned a ballet starring John Martin-Harvey as the Queen. Publicity for *Lilies* tapped into the dizziness of the plot: there was a conspiracy of secrecy to build up the surprise of Meggie's showstopping entrance in a crinoline. An interview with

---

[207] *Seven Ages,* 192
[208] *Seven Ages,* 196
[209] J. Hastings Turner, *The Lilies of the Field* (Blackwell, Oxford 1923), 27

Pall Mall during rehearsals began, characteristically, with her relief at being in work again, but ended with a flirtatious little trailer of 'Ah, the dresses!'[210]

Meggie liked Best, whose twin babies sometimes livened up rehearsals; cast for contrast, they played up to it, posing for photographers with blonde and brunette heads close together and developing a double act of friendly rivalry in public. They went to see the debut of Fred and Adele Astaire in *Stop Flirting!* The *Yorkshire Express* noted that they looked like 'the best of pals…as if chocolate wouldn't melt in their mouths.'[211] The rapport meant they could anticipate each other's cues and gave a sparkle of in-jokiness to some of their exchanges.

Lilies was a family comedy depending on teamwork rather than putting the strain on individuals. As well as the rising star Best there were vintage performers who comprised a comedy master class. The vicar was J.H. Roberts, who had the most delicately ironic lines and carried off some of the best notices. The grandmother was Gertrude Kingston, a cosmopolitan and eccentric presence. Sargent and Sickert had painted her, Shaw wrote *The Great Catherine* for her and she campaigned strenuously for the Conservatives because she felt Lloyd George had betrayed the cause of female suffrage. (Dean forgave the Toryism because she was a disciple of Reinhardt and had been the first manager in the country to install a proper system of dimmers.)

The play was full of comic opportunities for Meggie. It let her use both Terry melodrama and Du Maurier mockery. She sent up Victorian drama in gorgeous costumes and revoltingly sentimental poses: she knelt trustingly at her father's feet, lowered her eyes in horror when the word 'breeches' was uttered, swept curtseys and danced a quadrille. She also commanded the climax of the play, when she ripped off her crinoline in a fury of honesty, confronting her starchy lover (Austin Trevor), as she stood tiny and belligerent in a hoop and frilly drawers.

Dean hoped it was an opportunity to 'let her hair down' and enjoy herself. It was the only role so far to exploit her vibrant physicality, allowing her to dance across two centuries. The lively characterisation meant that she did not carry the weight of the play as she had done in *East of Suez*, while the audience laughter still provided an instant indication that she was getting the effects she desired. 'The delight of the audience seemed to float about the theatre in waves,' Dean recalled.[212] A love poem to 'the flimsy crinoline of Meggie Albanesi' appeared in the next ReandeaN newsletter.

It was a silly play, but it also touched on the idea of female identity. Gertrude Kingston brought a tartness to her role that sprang from her own feminism, ironising her lines to suggest that the older generation did not hanker unreservedly for 'the good old days'. Meggie followed this line of thought: she let the character's worries about disillusioning her lover be real rather than a mere second act complication, darkening the action with what the *Bystander* considered 'a strange power'.[213] 'She manages,' noted the *Daily Herald,* 'with one of her supremely beautiful hand gestures, to create a tense emotional atmosphere.'[214]

The complexity she found saved a sagging spot in the play's construction (as the sound of the robots next door blowing up the factory echoed through the Ambassadors, people sometimes remarked 'another critic'). But it also invited the

[210] *Pall Mall*, 2 June 1923
[211] *Yorkshire Express*, 1 June 1923
[212] *Seven Ages*, 194
[213] *Bystander*, 4 July 1923
[214] *Daily Herald*, 6 June 1923

post-war young to consider media-created identities like 'flapper' or 'Bright Young Thing' and decide what they thought of them. It challenged them to think how they differed from their mothers, and whether they were glad to do so. Meggie's challenge in her 'minx' outfit, 'This is me!',[215] allowed them to understand the scatty flapper as they understood Sydney Fairfield, as a person building a self in a difficult world. The social-realist playwright Charles McEvoy , a ReandeaN writer, explored the naturalism of the new generation, which he found exemplified in *Lilies* as much as in his own starker plays. He noted that younger actors were expected to have an understanding of psychology far beyond that demanded of the actors of fifty years ago. The 'intimate entertainment' of *Lilies,* he thought, was not only a credit to them, but to the audience prepared to make the journey with them. Both sides, he felt, were committed to a more rewarding theatre than 'the charm of Miss Albanesi …sacrificed to the game of getting every ounce of traditional stage "jam" out of Lady Teazle'.[216]

ReandeaN was in the fortunate position of having two successes at a point when many theatres were in despair. It was the hottest summer on record. The *R.U.R.* cast suffered in their robot costumes, London was airless and audiences often torpid. Meggie, boiling in her crinoline, used to slip out of her basement dressing room to smoke in the fresh air and chat to the children from the tenements, a little bemused when a five-year-old demanded a cigarette. *R.U.R.* was replaced by McEvoy's *The Likes of 'er,* but *Lilies* continued to fill houses throughout the heatwave. (It was an engagement treat for the Duke of York and Lady Elizabeth Bowes-Lyon, the royal event of the year.) The success probably helped the reconciliation between Meggie and Dean.

He took her to lunch at the Carlton Grill and they talked about the future in terms that would stretch the company. He mentioned Juliet; she was shy about her looks, but had studied the part with Kate Rorke, a friend since *Spectacles*, whose verse-speaking Shaw had praised. They considered Nora in *A Doll's House*, and hoped for better translations of Chekhov. They broke off when she realised she was late for her voice class and took a taxi up the Haymarket. They kissed, and the kiss escalated, until they were on the verge of a plan to go away together. The taxi driver complained, and she rushed off to her lesson in distress.

The next day they backed off. There is no record of what Meggie thought of the encounter or how large a space it occupied in her emotional landscape. For Dean it mattered, and the kiss in the taxi takes up a poignant amount of space in an autobiography that is often perfunctory about personal relationships. He was convinced that she was still in love with Owen Nares, and might be settling for him out of what he describes as 'a deeply felt need for her own sexual regulation'.[217] The phrase is so clumsy it seems equally charged with good intentions, wounded feelings and potential to destroy any hope of a successful outcome. His passion, he concluded at the time, showed a desire to keep Meggie's career on track; later, he wondered with sad humility whether 'she might have similar aims regarding myself'.

This is quite possible. The relief at her return had shown her that the company saw her as its moving spirit. She might have been beginning to reflect on policy. Dean had sometimes been timid in his choices and their mutual interest in

---

[215] Turner, *Lilies of the Field*, 116
[216] ReandeaN Newssheet Vol I no. 6
[217] *Seven Ages*, 197

Ibsen and Chekhov might have led her to encourage bolder projects. He visited Moscow not long after her death, but if he had done so while she was still binding ReandeaN together they might have achieved something extraordinary. Although they never followed through that episode in the taxi it cleared the air; there was a bond of real affection between them and the arguments stopped.

There were other signs that she was moving on. If she was still lacking confidence in her talent she was finding strategies to develop it. She took up the piano again and taught herself some Scriabin preludes as a surprise for Carlo. He felt that she had improved out of all measure: the ghost of her failure at the Royal Academy of Music was laid, and she continued to play. She went to lectures on the History of the Drama, part of RADA's new diploma course in conjunction with London University. She took extensive notes in an exercise book and dropped in several times to discuss plays with Kenneth Barnes: this suggests she was mulling over Dean's idea that she might work on classic roles. She also seemed to be taking her health more seriously; she bought a car and made trips to the country; at weekends she took the midnight train to Broadstairs, often with Lorn Macnaughtan; the Kingsgate Castle Hotel welcomed her as a regular.

She began to study Italian – mostly to please Carlo, although with the Fascists newly in power in Italy she might have wanted to think out what her inheritance meant to her. There was a further incentive. In 1921 Duse was touring Europe. In 1923 there were several opportunities in England to see her in one of her most famous parts, Mrs Alving in *Ghosts,* performed, like all her roles, in Italian. Young actors were especially drawn to Duse. They knew about her by hearsay; when most of them were still children she had withdrawn from the stage to spend twelve years in study, especially of the mystics. Now in her sixties, she was frail and her hair had turned white; she refused to wear make-up or change her appearance. Consistently, though, her audience was overwhelmed by the truth of her playing.

Duse's understanding of the art of performance as an essentially religious act was attractive to the first drama school generation. Courses like Meggie's RADA lectures ensured that they knew the religious origins of theatre. *Kenosis,* the emptying of the self, was the cornerstone of her art; as Ibsen's friend Bang wrote, 'Duse's power of mental concentration is unequalled. It is not only the very essence of her art; it is also – and this is what makes her unique – the only means she uses.'[218]

Meggie was compared to many major performers, especially after her death, but the name that recurred most often was that of Duse. It was not a comparison she would have presumed to accept: but her own capacity for silence and stillness as the way to beckon her audience in would have drawn her to Duse as a model . Her approach was closer to Meggie's aspirations than those of the other major performers at the close of their acting lives, Bernhardt and Terry.

At last, the Playbox was up and running in the scorching and stormy July of 1923. The first play was Masefield's *Melloney Holtspur, or the Pangs of Love*, a ghost story about love and betrayal with overtones of *The Winter's Tale* and *Wuthering Heights.* Masefield had written it before 1914, but it had a new resonance for a generation betrayed into war and then unemployment. Meggie played Lenda, the young woman whose happiness depends on reconciliation between two ghosts – her father, artist, thief and seducer Lonnie Copshrews, and Melloney, the girl he loved and left to die of grief, now trying to prevent a marriage between Lenda and

[218] Quoted in Eva Le Gallienne, *Eleonora Duse: The Mystic in the Theatre* (Bodley Head NY 1965), 12

her nephew Bunny. In their modern clothes, their ease with motorcars and their refusal to join the feuds of the older generation, Lenda and Bunny seemed to lay the ghosts of recent history.

The real star of the production was Dean's new Schwabe-Hasait lighting system. Spectres in mould-coloured make-up and black veils walked through walls; clouds loomed and lightning flashed; a suit of armour came periodically to life and made gnomic pronouncements; moonlight gave way to dawn and both dissolved into flashbacks, dream sequences and encounters between the dead and the living (all on a modest budget). Some felt Dean was acting like a boy with a new train set; some disparaged Masefield's uncertain handling of stage conventions and awkward dialogue (Meggie had to address her lover as 'My Little Bunny'). But the production stimulated debate and confirmed ReandeaN's status as a theatre of ideas. The *Evening Standard* was disturbed by Masefield's existentialist image of the afterlife, professing itself shocked at his presentation of the virginal Melloney as a tortured spirit while the ghosts of two of Lonny's unchaste but forgiving victims were shown 'dancing in blue and gold'.[219]

When someone asks Lenda what her name means, she says, 'It means me.'[220] J.T. Grein wrote of Meggie that 'she dominated by her unconscious assertion of "I am I."'[221] This was not a criticism that she could only play herself, still less that she used a role to indulge her ego; rather, it implied that her power lay in the way she gave her audience a self wholly engaged in the act of performing. Lenda is not a naturalistic character; she has no quirks or mannerisms to make her 'real', nor does she experience growth or change. Like Perdita in *The Winter's Tale* she exists as a symbolic function. Lenda has to draw the audience into the play as ritual of redemption. At the climax she is surrounded by spirits, vengeful and the blessed, a lightning rod for the forces at work in the play; she has few lines but it is crucial that she remains the focal point, because she initiates the chain of forgiveness, which resolves the action.

Despite their other reservations the critics responded to Meggie's Lenda; they admired her willingness not to obtrude with 'characterisation', to 'that queer, still power of emotional intensity of hers which makes all her work seem so clean-cut and effortless and devoid of fuss.'[222] The Playbox organised a debate with Marie Tempest in the chair which the cast must have found diverting. Conal O'Riordan announced it was the most boring ghost play ever, 'except one' – Earl Russell, recumbent on a prop sofa, languidly identified that one as *Hamlet.* The ReandeaN newsletter recorded the comment of one member of the audience on Masefield, 'I find his sex complex too simple.'[223] It was a successful fortnight, although the combination of *Lilies* and *Melloney* meant Meggie was giving eleven performances a week. Masefield wrote to her,'You are going to be the wonder of our stage.'[224]

Her health was getting worse; she had even considered backing out of *Melloney*: but the box office needed her and her emotional investment in the Playbox was too great. It was also a chance to prove herself in a very different dramatic register, one she might otherwise have missed, for Dean was unable to include her in his next project. At last, after ten years, he was going to open *Hassan*

---

219 *Evening Standard,* 11 July 1923
220 John Masefield, *Melloney Holtspur,* (Heinemann 1922), 76
221 *Sketch,* 16 Dec 1923
222 *Daily Telegraph,* 11 July 1923
223 ReandeaN Newssheet Vol 1 no. 4
224 *Meggie Albanesi,* 131

in September. He had the theatre – His Majesty's – where he had originally hoped to stage it with Tree in 1913; original music was commissioned from Delius; Fokine was putting the dancers through an intensive training that established traditions in British ballet for years to come. George Harris had his biggest budget ever. The cast included ReandeaN regulars, including Malcolm Keen, and would have reunited Meggie with Henry Ainley and the Shrimp; on Meggie's recommendation Drake was understudying Cathleen Nesbitt, pregnant with what Asquith dubbed 'Liberal baby of the year'.

Almost since they met Dean had envisaged Meggie as Pervaneh. The role brings intimate intensity to the play after its spectacular scenes. Pervaneh has to decide whether she and her lover will part and live, or be tortured to death after a single day of love. She demands death with fanatical passion; later, she appears as a ghost, aghast that the wraith of her lover seems to have forgotten everything. Like the opium speech in *East of Suez,* it requires a performer with the charisma to lead the audience beyond realism and into ritual.

Hassan was going to be the play of the year . Dean felt, however, that he owed it to Alec Rea to keep Meggie in *Lilies,* frustrating as this might be for them both. The critical and commercial success of *Hassan* did not altogether make up for his disappointment: while full of praise for the male performers he felt that Laura Cowie, his Melloney Holtspur, was not well cast as Pervaneh. This may not have been a fault of her playing. The play has the vivid stylisation of the Arabian Nights but the female parts are constructed as erotic spectacle – in the case of Pervaneh, sadistic spectacle. Dean correctly pointed out to the censor that nothing is shown; but the torture of Pervaneh is framed by descriptions, by tableaux of the executioner in silhouette, by onstage reactions to things allegedly too terrible to speak aloud.

I am not attempting to criticise Dean or Laura Cowie for failing to construct a feminist or post-colonial reading of the play: rather, I would suggest that, like *East of Suez,* the text makes demands on the female performer that are mutually contradictory. Meggie's performance might have satisfied Dean better than Cowie's; but it probably would not have satisfied her. Lenda, although a more subdued role, was a better stepping stone to Shakespeare. It not only confirmed her ability to work in a non-naturalistic style. It also established that the 'modernity' for which she had always been praised did not indicate a limited range or a need for texts with specifically twenties' mannerisms and language. It proved that it was a function of her approach to any role, avoiding McEvoy's 'stage jam' of accumulated tradition and bringing a contemporary sensibility to bear on it.

With *Hassan* running, Dean let himself be persuaded into a partnership with Alfred Butt at the Queen's. The first production was *The Little Minister* with Fay Compton and Owen Nares, opening on 7 November. If this stirred up uncomfortable memories (at one point the *Morning Post*, remembering *The First and the Last*, ran an article directly comparing Compton and Albanesi) Dean never discussed it. With *Lilies* still packing the Ambassadors in the chilly autumn, he arranged a new Playbox venture for Meggie, an adaptation of Vincent Brown's novel *A Magdalen's Husband.* Dean had no illusions about the play: it had stereotyped characters and its comedy was stolid. But Meggie was drawn to the part of Joan, a young woman forced to leave her village after a sexual peccadillo, who returns to marry the drunken and violent Martin as a self-imposed penance. A young gardener, Zeekel, kills Martin to protect Joan; another man is tried for the murder, but Joan realises the truth and persuades Zeekel to give himself up. The play ends as she and Zeekel's brother sit together on the morning of his execution.

The year 1922 had seen the trial of Edith Thompson and Frederick Bywaters for the murder of Thompson's husband. Thompson had not participated in the killing; there was grave doubt about the degree of her involvement at any level. When both were found guilty there was widespread pressure for her reprieve; but the lovers were hanged in January 1923. The case haunted the public imagination. It raised hard questions about female desire, complicity, justice and power. *A Magdalen's Husband* confronted these questions with surprising boldness. The censor appears at one point to have demanded an alternative ending in which Zeekel survives, although the rewrites are deleted in the version of the play lodged with the Lord Chamberlain. Dean can have been in no doubt that the play would spark controversies about justice and gender even fiercer than the debates over *Bill* and *Loyalties*.

Joan herself is a character with blazing religious certainty but also a feminist independence that leads her to storm out of Martin's house. She may have things in common with Hardy's Tess but the play is firmly located in the post-war world; if her sexual choices are grounded in an older morality they are not taken for granted, and the actress has opportunities to show the process by which she reaches them. On the stage of the twenties it was impossible to show domestic abuse directly but it is always clear how violent Martin can be; at the same time the text endows him with a bewildered longing for some warmth, some weakness in Joan that might make their relationship less arid.

In the scenes between Martin and Joan there is the possibility of a fire Meggie had not been able to show since she played Sydney. Dean, fresh from the social realism of MacEvoy's *The Likes of 'er*, expressed doubts – not to Meggie's face – as to whether the part was in her range. He thought she might be too middle-class – 'an orchid can't play a cabbage.'[225] She challenged that description; perhaps the role Dane had written for her helped her to identify the feminist passion of Joan. Rehearsals convinced Dean that she seemed to be on the verge of 'another giant stride forward'.[226]

She was increasingly tired, and visiting the doctor frequently. Her family remembered her at this time as happy, however, and she was seeing a lot of them. On her birthday in October she had, as she said, 'a gorgeous day' and asked her parents to help refurbish her flat in New Cavendish Street. Effie commandeered a housekeeper and organised friends to fill the bookshelves. (Sentimentally, she saw Meggie's current craze for Harrison Ainsworth as a sign she was turning away from 'pernicious literature', although it probably just indicated that historical cliffhangers were easier dressing room reading than *Ulysses*.) Carlo hung prints he had chosen for Meggie out of his collection. She made his birthday a month later a gala event at the Embassy Club, with Michael Arlen at the party.

The happiness was perhaps an indication of her growing confidence as a performer and company member. She was in touch with Dane, and they had hopes that *The Way Things Happen* would not be postponed much longer. She saw Barrie dining alone at the Ivy. When she approached him he asked her to come and visit: he had a play in mind for her. She was the first person to book tickets for the annual RADA dinner on 8 December, proud that she was still technically a student by virtue of the diploma course. She had new photographs taken to sign for her fans.

Throughout the autumn J.T.Grein's theatre column in the *Illustrated London*

---

[225] Edward Percy, quoted in *Meggie Albanesi,* 160
[226] *Seven Ages*, 216

News had been preoccupied with the state of English acting. Despite the current lack of Irvings he thought standards were rising; his sentiments were much the same as McEvoy's. 'The rank and file are splendid...we demand of our actors nowadays that they should not only impersonate, but penetrate, their parts.'[227] On 3 November Grein launched a debate. It was an attempt to push the analysis of acting beyond the standard British text on the psychology of performance, Archer's *Masks or Faces?*, which was now thirty-five years old. Citing Coquelin's remark on technique – that he could think of something quite different while performing – Grein sought opinions from the profession. He noted that they now possessed intellectual force and freedom, that 'no actor is afraid nowadays to take part in public discussions, even if his views are in flagrant contradiction to those of managers and critics.'[228]

Matheson Lang responded the following week with nostalgia for the 'old Bohemian actor'. He accused modern players of being too respectable. 'The lives they lead are too conventional, too regulated, too like the lives of the business and social world, where feelings are hidden away beneath the mask of everyday conventional life.'[229] It was not the change in moral standards that bothered him, but the way actors mixed in society rather than remaining apart – the cost, Lang thought, would be the sacrifice of physical expressiveness in order to fit in.

Meggie's generation, who had learned from the Langs and the Du Mauriers, did not lack the physical resources of the Bohemians, but for many of them the body had to be driven by the character's emotion, not vice versa. Meggie weighed in the following week, alongside contributions from Yvonne Arnaud, Denis Neilson-Terry, Fred Wright and Ivor Novello.

> You ask me whether or not an actor should feel his own emotions affected by the part he is portraying. It is, as you say, an old problem, and one to which it will always be impossible to give a definite answer. In my opinion, it is not possible sincerely to convey to the audience any emotion which one does not feel, to some extent, within oneself. The brain may suggest expressions and acting suitable to the situation, but without some real feeling surely there will be something lacking. At the same time, while an actor should feel his part, I think his feelings should be under his control, rather than be allowed to gain control of him. When players lose control of themselves, they lose control of their audience. The power of feeling is a gift. The actor is lucky who possesses it and can use it with restraint and judgement, as all gifts should be used. These are, as clearly as I can put them, my views on this always most interesting question.[230]

She asked questions in rehearsal, she talked about theatre with everyone she ever worked with, but this was her only venture into print. She did not have much gift for writing – Eva was the one who had wanted to emulate Effie – but to join this debate was to assume a particular authority: not the right to define acting, but the right to join the search for a definition.

She was also defining herself. In 1921, newly successful, she had described

---

[227] J.T.Grein, *Illustrated London News*, 22 Sept 1923
[228] J.T.Grein, *Illustrated London News*, 3 Nov 1923
[229] Matheson Lang, *Illustrated London News,* 24 Nov 1923
[230] Meggie Albanesi, *Illustrated London News,* 1 Dec 1923

herself in much simpler terms, as 'one of those actresses who suffer each time.'[231] Now her understanding of the process was more complex. For her, the difference did not lie in the process of delivery; an actor was not distinguished by the way he or she expressed onstage emotions that are common to everyone. Rather, an actor's feelings had a quality unique to performers; feelings were in themselves a gift, which technique could direct. Like most people attempting to theorize a creative process she found it difficult to verbalise how the actor controlled both self and audience, but there was no self-deprecation in her answer.

The Sunday after her letter was printed, her parents came to tea in the flat; she was packing Christmas presents for Eva's children and gave Effie and Carlo copies of the new photographs; compared to the vital images of her in *Lilies* they seem lacking in animation. This may reflect her extreme tiredness, or, perhaps, like those earlier fashion pictures, her need for work to bring her fully to life.

There is another image from this time. While there are no photographs of her as Joan, George Harris's design for *A Magdalen's Husband* survives. It is a beautifully painted watercolour of a rustic kitchen with only one window to give light, the only colour a scarlet cloth on the table at which Joan will sit to read the Bible. There is a figure in the painting, wearing a brown dress. Slightly more than life size in comparison with the surroundings, it stands rooted firm, alert; the hands are large, worker's hands, unmistakably Meggie's. Her vitality, it seems, was a given, as soon as the play began to take shape in the company's imagination.

She felt Joan was a watershed role. She told Hannen Swaffer that she had not progressed since *Bill of Divorcement* and added, 'If I am no better in *A Magdalen's Husband* I shall know I shall not go far.' But this does not sound like the anticipation of failure; she chose, after all, to say it to a journalist. In private there was no self-reproach, perhaps because her work in rehearsal was now reaching a standard even she could sense was different. Dean hardly ever praised actors till the first night; this time he not only did so but was visibly moved to tears by the last scene. The fear, instead, was that she might not be well enough to play.

She confided it to Effie, recalling the illnesses that had dogged her first nights since she played Lady Teazle. 'I have great luck,' she commented, 'but I'm not lucky.'[232] The day after her parents' visit she was at Ciro's with a tall, military-looking man, laughing at the way they appeared on the dance floor. Several journalists there noted how pale she was. 'You'll kill yourself if you're not careful,'[233] said one.

On Wednesday she went to a matinee of Sutton Vane's *Outward Bound.* She found it disturbing, she told Effie. It is the story of a group of passengers on a ship which proves to be heading for the afterlife. In a kind of inverted version of *The First and the Last* a pair of suicidal lovers get the chance to live again, to wake up and turn off the gas. That night she was visibly ill during *Lilies,* her voice so hoarse she could hardly speak; she would not take a curtain call and wept in her dresser's arms. Gertrude Kingston recalled comforting her in her dressing-room as she expressed her fear that she would let down the cast of *Magdalen's Husband.*

She told Dean about the fear following the last magical run-though. He recalled this as a rehearsal which moved the whole cast onto a new acting level and left them unwilling to leave until they had seen her in the closing moments, reading John's Gospel.

---

[231] *Weekly Dispatch,* 5 June 1921
[232] *Meggie Albanesi,*163
[233] *Daily Graphic,* 10 Dec 1923

> Gradually the quiet, slightly hoarse voice began to pour its emotion over us, as the pupils of her eyes dilated, making them seem twice their normal size, and the whole personality became charged with explosive force. The effect was shattering. There was silence for a full minute after the curtain fell, and then spontaneous applause burst from the little knot of actors. Then they filed quietly out of the theatre, humbled in the face of a unique experience.'[234]

Edward Percy, who had dramatised the novel for Dean, later shared with Effie his own recollection of 'St John's glorious simplicities in that queer, husky voice which plucked so sharply at one's heart and was so cruelly near to its last silence...it was as if her soul were shining through her body.'[235]

Dean went to her dressing room. She threw her arms round him and cried. He was used to her tears at the end of a performance, but they were usually because she thought she had failed. This time she thought she would never play the part.

It was the last time he saw her on stage.* He met her at the Ivy. Her face had a greenish tint that frightened him. He promised to put her understudy on for the rest of the week. Effie met her at the flat, excited by the prospect of a long weekend in Broadstairs to recover; she would go alone, she said, to rest her voice. The weather was freezing; she planned to do nothing more energetic than look out of the window at the sea. On the train a woman passenger saw she was in pain and haemorrhaging badly; the passenger called the guard and improvised a bed. The night bus from the Kingsgate Castle came to meet her but her Good Samaritan took her into her own house and called a doctor, who moved her straight into the South Court Nursing Home. He rang Meggie's doctor, who in turn called Effie, but Meggie insisted she should be spared the details. Effie and Lorn went down the next day, on the same train as the surgeon called to operate.

This time, however, there was no real hope of success; the surgeon later confided to Dean that he had been shocked by her condition and could not imagine how she had managed to go on working. Effie telephoned Carlo, who reached Broadstairs on Sunday morning and summoned a priest. Carlo and Meggie had a short, cheerful conversation in Italian; she asked for Effie, and then she slipped away from them both.

The Playbox matinee had been scheduled for the Tuesday afternoon. That day the entire company signed a letter to Dean offering sympathy and expressing their willingness 'to help in all ways to make things as easy for you as possible'. It remains in his personal archives; every name is marked with a tick, suggesting that at some time he tried to thank each one of them.

The requiem mass took place on 14 December at St James's, Spanish Place, the old and beautiful Catholic Church near her flat in New Cavendish Street. The plain coffin under the golden angel roof carried a wreath of rosemary from her parents tied with blue ribbon. The church was filled with flowers; there were two

---

[234] *Seven Ages,* 167

[235] *Meggie Albanesi*, 161

* Dean places the last rehearsal on the Thursday morning. According to Effie her daughter was too ill to play that day and went to the theatre only to ask Dean for some time off. She places that last runthrough earlier, but is vague about the date, although she recalls Meggie's joy at what was evidently a breakthrough performance. I am inclined to follow Dean here because the rehearsal timetable seems to make sense and agrees with the newspapers who reported on events at the time. But both Dean and Effie's accounts seem primarily motivated by a desire to envisage her doing what made her happiest on her last day.

hundred wreaths from theatres alone. The whole ReandeaN company and crew were there; the St Martin's remained dark the whole day. There were actors from every theatre in London, from RADA; the church was not big enough to hold them all.

They laid her in St Pancras Roman Catholic Cemetery in Finchley. Dean hung back until everyone had left; then he stood for a long time at her grave. Afterwards he left London for days.

Curtain

We sit on a darkened stage, with a lowered curtain,
Neighbours of death. And yet it is she who dies.
She that was young…
Nay, there's no more to be said
Only a song unsung
Only a script unread.[236]

(W.T. Titterton, in the ReandeaN News Sheet)

There were so many projects left undone. When Duse died the following year she was mourned; but her audience had already thought through her acting life in their minds. The critics were poised to weigh the memory of one performance against another, to consider her as a youthful Juliet and an elderly Mrs Alving and sum up a talent that had fulfilled itself. In Meggie's case the response was different. The age had become accustomed to the deaths of the young and brilliant: Rupert Brooke was mentioned more than once in her obituaries. The critics strove to pack into short paragraphs not only what she had achieved, but to imagine the future contexts her unique talent might have made for itself.

There were different emphases. Some saw her work as limited, for others her potential was boundless, the only limitation that of her short life. Some discussed technique, some felt that she had no need of it. The words that recur again and again, however, are words concerned with energy. James Douglas saw her as Blake's Tyger; John Hastings Turner, in a more homely spirit, as a terrier. Both fit the fencing champion, the passionate dancer, the indefatigable rehearser. Other images, though, depend less on the sense of her body in action; they speak of light, warmth, glow, fire. Beyond any conception of individual roles, she was a source of power.

For a long time, Meggie was an absent presence at the St Martin's. *A Magdalen's Husband* opened in January with Moyna Macgill as Joan, to reviews largely occupied with the performance not taking place. Christopher St John suggested that 'the dreariness of the acting was more real than feigned'[237] because of grief, and devoted her review to an evaluation of Meggie. John Francis Hope's review in *The New Age* was cruel to Macgill with the anger of the bereaved. 'The first (sob) day of the week (grizzle) cometh (hoo! hoo!) Mary Magda (hoo! hoo!) lene early….. I regretted the death of Meggie Albanesi during the performance.'[238]

The First ReandeaN Gala Evening, a free gift to reward Playbox subscribers, was, Dean considered, 'lifeless', even Sybil Thorndike's power damped by the loss. The London run of *Lilies* ended in February and the play went on tour with Best in Meggie's part. She wrote to Effie that she often sensed her presence at moments in the play they had enjoyed.

---

[236] W.T.Titterton, *Daily News*, 14 Dec 1923
[237] *Time and Tide*, 18 Jan 1924
[238] *The New Age*, 10 Jan 1924

The Way Things Happen was scheduled to open in February and Hilda Bayley played the role written for Meggie. Clemence Dane's stage directions confirm that Shirley was 'she and no other':

> A girl of 20 or thereabouts…she is pale, dark-eyed, and not good-looking until she smiles. People generally think of her as 'a queer little thing' and yet she is not so little, is sturdily built indeed, with erect carriage and capable, work-stained hands. She moves deftly…she reminds you of a born dreamer who is never allowed a good night's sleep. ..her manner is either so impassive and suppressed as to make you think her stupid, or as vehement as the little kettle boiling over on the hearth.[239]

The play is a feminist take on *Measure for Measure*. Shirley is in love with a man who treats her like a sister; when he is discovered 'borrowing' some bonds, she tries to save him by sleeping with his employer. The emphasis however, is not on her dilemma but its aftermath. It contrasts his petulant inability to cope with what she has done and why with the developing bond of affection between Shirley and his mother.

Dane and Meggie had discussions during the development of the script. The role needed her clarity and integrity to support its project of undermining Edwardian preconceptions. Like *Lilies* the text explored relationships between women, an opportunity for the company to explore a different dramatic chemistry. Without Meggie as a box office draw, however, the gender balance was seen as a disadvantage. *The Times* sniffed that only the predominance of women in the audience caused it to be 'enthusiastically received'.[240] Bayley could not hold the production together and it had only a short run.

There were other ReandeaN projects less far advanced. Playbox publicity had listed Coward's *The Rat Trap* as one of its future productions. It never came to fruition – in his autobiography Dean seems to have forgotten it altogether – but Coward dedicated the published edition to Meggie. Given that like many of his plays it contained 'a whacking good part' for himself, it might have offered a chance to see the two of them together. It would have been a combination of talents very different from Coward's other famous partnerships. Exploring a marriage of writers in which gender roles, unequal talents and commercial success make a volatile mix, it needed a more intellectual style of comedy than that of Gertrude Lawrence; the comedy of envy echoed *Design for Living* but while in that play Coward and the Lunts achieved the rapport of three characters who think alike, *Rat Trap* needed a spiky difference of styles, one that actors as different in background and outlook as Meggie and Coward could have brought to it. It also had fiery quarrels to which only close friends could really do justice.

Barrie wrote to Effie 'That talk I was to have with her was to be about a part I expect I shall never write now.'[241] Meggie had a special admiration for his work; she told Effie she wanted to play Wendy in *Peter Pan*; the play was a childhood favourite, but the painful relationship between the eternal boy and the girl 'too loving to be ignorant that he is not loving enough'[242] would have appealed to her

---

[239] Clemence Dane, *The Way Things Happen* (Heinemann 1924), 2–3
[240] *The Times*, 4 Feb 1924
[241] *Meggie Albanesi*, 187
[242] J.M.Barrie, *Peter Pan*, in *Collected Plays* (Hodder and Stoughton 1928), 64

adult intelligence. She now had the experience she had lacked at the time of *Dear Brutus*. Barrie's complex and original analysis of sexual dynamics would have given her a further chance to grow. These unfinished projects suggest that her energy might have driven a feminist repertoire within ReandeaN that only societies like the Pioneers could have matched.

The company said its farewell to Meggie on 9 July 1924, with a matinee to raise funds for a RADA scholarship. ReandeaN actors from every production she had worked on performed sketches. Barrie wrote one specially. Henry Ainley recited Flecker. There were performers from other theatre worlds – Jack Buchanan and June, the Astaires, George Robey – and friends like Betty Chester and the Shrimp. The RADA ballet class danced. Others sold programmes and acted as ushers, including Viola Tree, C. Aubrey Smith and Alec Rea. Gertrude Lawrence organised a midnight performance of Charlot's revue in New York to raise an equivalent amount. They made more than £1600, enough for a scholarship, which is still available to students. The first winner was Jean Shepheard, an orphan supporting herself by working as a typist. She was small and dark and plain and reminded the judges of Meggie.

ReandeaN was in difficulties. Following Meggie's death there were successes, but also disasters; there were no more periods of stability like the runs of *Bill* or *Loyalties* or *Lilies*. The Playbox was abandoned for lack of funds; in an interview with W.T Titterton for the newssheet Dean said that 'the pressure began at the time when we lost our own brightest star – dear Meggie Albanesi.'[243]

In 1925 Alec Rea announced that he did not want to go on financing the venture. Dean continued to draw upon the group of talented actors he brought together, but the distinctive ReandeaN identity was gone and its special audience with it. There was no single reason for the break-up. Dean felt he had made some poor choices, but he was also the victim of bad luck. Alec Rea had been close to Dean's first wife, and was losing his sense of the enterprise as a family concern: more conservative in his dramatic tastes than Dean, he was increasingly reluctant to support Dean's challenges to the censor. There would have been strains in any event: but a performer of Meggie's brilliance and box office appeal would have made a vast difference to the company's prospects. The sheer affection in which Dean, Rea and the whole company held her – and her emotional investment in them – might have eased some of the tensions.

For her relationship with ReandeaN was unique. As her obituaries pointed out, she was famous in a new way.[244] Her roles were not the kind a young actress would have taken even a few years previously. 'She was modernity,'[245] said one. 'The genius of her age and time,'[246] said another. She had constructed a performing self from the best of the Victorian tradition and the energy and experiment of dynamic women practitioners like Craig, McCarthy and Dane. ReandeaN provided a context in which she could develop and communicate it. She recognised her debt to Dean and more than once spoke of her luck and what she had learned from him; this was, as he recognised, not a one-way process. Looking back, he saw her impact as formative, remarking that until they worked together he 'held no particular views on the problems of either acting or production. It was only after the loss of Meggie

[243] ReandeaN News Sheet Vol 2 no. 5
[244] *Daily News*, 12 July 1924
[245] *Sphere*, 22 Dec 1923
[246] *The Weekly Westminster*, 15 Dec 1923

that I began consciously to direct my thought towards developing the technique of the ensemble.'[247]

Both did themselves less than justice. Dean did not teach her to act, he did not need to; but the working conditions he created were unparalleled. She was with people who wanted to discuss and experiment, who believed in the totality of the theatrical experience and the importance of everyone who contributed to it. She had an audience who, increasingly, did not just applaud but found in ReandeaN a forum where their comments were expected and taken seriously and where the company would answer back. Any director could have made her a star. Dean made her a leader. This was not a position of privilege, and colleagues evidently realised that; it explains the phenomenon on which so many of her obituaries remarked, the willingness right through the profession to give her help and advice. It was, rather, a position of danger; she could transmit her energy and her passion to the company, but the responsibility she felt led her to risk herself, as she did in that early return to *Lilies*, or to blame herself for flaws not of her making, as in *East of Suez.*

It was a position uniquely exposed. Other actors had been and would continue to be lucky enough to enter companies that nourished them; but not in the glare of the West End with untried plays to carry on their shoulders. ReandeaN occupied a space between the commercial and the avant-garde that would not be filled again. The generation a few years younger, Gielgud, Olivier, Ashcroft, would earn in one sphere and learn in the other.

But that exposure also provided her with the unique pleasure of creating new roles in new work. At her death, some wondered if this was a limitation and pointed out that she had not yet performed any of the classic roles, while Agate complained that she 'refrained' from Ibsen and Chekhov.[248] This last is unfair: at the time Agate himself was the only critic in England to champion Chekhov and the following year Gielgud made his debut as Trofimov in a production received with bewildered incomprehension. Chekhov would have been part of her modernity, as would the plays in which Coward defined the later twenties. If she had shared the long lifespans of the rest of the great generation, she might have responded more swiftly than most of them to the post-1956 playwrights.

Throughout his lifetime Dean continued to express his awareness of her absent presence. He stayed in touch with the family, offering Eva walk-on parts to ease her financial difficulties in the face of her final split with Marshall. Effie sent some first-night good wishes and he offered material for the biography she began to write after the death of Carlo, who had not long survived the loss of his daughter. 'This knowledge that she is still loved and remembered,' she wrote to him in 1927, 'is one of the few gleams of light in a life which since I lost my beloved husband is terribly desolate and bleak.'[249]

As extracts from the biography appeared in the press, Dean became defensive: he felt that he was being accused of causing Meggie's death through overwork and wrote to Effie, 'I mourn her loss with almost every play that I am called upon to cast. Can you not see that any suggestion that our association was other than the quick sympathy of two enthusiastic artists (not that of a selfish manager and an over-worked actress) causes me deep pain?'[250] Belatedly

[247] Dean, *Seven Ages*, 31
[248] *Sunday Times*, 16 Dec 1923
[249] 6 Sep 1927. From the Basil Dean Archive
[250] 3 Feb 1928. From the Basil Dean Archive

acknowledging the published text from Effie, he verged on the uncivil. 'Meggie's loss is so irreparable in the English theatre that to read about those early days at the St Martin's even now gives me no pleasure but a sense of shock.'[251]

The letter was dictated, and the brusque tone may reflect a struggle to speak rather than deliberate unkindness. Effie lived until 1936, but Dean waited until his own old age to discuss in print those aspects of Meggie's life of which he considered her mother unaware, or unable to speak.

In 1953 her image preoccupied him still. He tried to organise the removal of her memorial from the St Martin's to the new theatre at RADA; he told Lord Willoughby de Broke, who owned the building, that since the theatre was no longer leased by a producing manager it 'does not seem quite so appropriate to connect the memory of this wonderful young actress with the building'.[252]

He did not succeed, and perhaps it is right that he did not. Schools do not have ghosts, but theatres do. This is nothing to do with the supernatural. The point of theatre is to create memory. Real events lodge in the mind through the emotion they evoke: but the details of the most powerful recollections – the gestures, the words , the setting – can be hazy. Theatre makes memories by planting these things in the mind, making them into a whole that , although fiction , possesses a reality that cannot be forgotten.

In the year of that last runthrough of *A Magdalen's Husband*, Meggie's ADA friend Eva le Gallienne visited Duse. Duse gave her a book of prayers by St Thomas Aquinas.[253] There was a marker next to one which began 'Generous giver, give also to my body splendid clarity.' It was the clarity, the unique energy Meggie Albanesi brought to every role that fixed her in the minds of everyone who saw her; it is there in the words of all those who tried to set down in print the sound of her voice and the movement of her body, in the photographs where she seems about to move and speak. If her name is still inscribed in the space where she created so many of those memories, that is how it should be.

---

[251] 8 May 1928. From the Basil Dean Archive
[252] 8 Dec 1953. From the Basil Dean Archive DEA 1/1/40
[253] Eva le Gallienne, *Eleonora Duse* (my translation), 1

CHRONOLOGY

July 1917: Haymarket Theatre; Lucy in *A Pair of Spectacles*
Sept 1917: Jul 1918 Wyndham's; understudy in *Dear Brutus*
Autumn 1918: on tour as Marie de Belforet in *Henry of Navarre*
June 1919: Lyric Hammersmith; Sonia in *The Rising Sun*
June 1919: Kingsway; Eva in *St George and the Dragons*
Sept 1919: St James's Theatre; Alexandra in *Reparation*
Oct 1919: Queen's Theatre; Elise in *Napoleon*
Dec 1919: Court Theatre; Blanche Amber in *The Reprobate*
Jan 1920: Queen's Theatre; Elise Merridew in *Mr Todd's Experiment*
April 1920: St Martin's; Jill in *The Skin Game*
Dec 1920: Comedy; Elise Challoner in *The Charm School*
March 1921: St Martin's; Sydney in *A Bill of Divorcement*
May 1921: RADA; Rose in *Trelawney of the 'Wells'*
May 1921: Aldwych; Wanda in *The First and the Last*
March 1922: St Martin's; Mabel in *Loyalties*, Jane in *Shall We join the Ladies?*
Sept 1922: His Majesty's; Daisy in *East of Suez*
June 1923:Ambassadors; Elizabeth in *The Lilies of the Field*
July 1923 St Martin's; Lenda in *Melloney Holtspur*

INDEX